Lily White in Detroit

by

Cynthia Harrison

Lily White in Detroit

Cover Art by *RJ Morris*

The Wild Rose Press, Inc.
PO Box 708
Adams Basin, NY 14410-0708
Visit us at www.thewildrosepress.com

Publishing History
First Mainstream Mystery Edition, 2018
Print ISBN 978-1-5092-2175-2
Digital ISBN 978-1-5092-2176-9

Published in the United States of America

"You're okay. I'm here now," he called out to her.

He had no idea if she was back there alone or if she was being held hostage. He could see most of the front two rooms, living room and kitchen, from where he stood. He made his way toward the little bit of the kitchen out of view. Nobody. Nobody in the hall either. He stepped deliberately, his weapon ready. Bathroom clear. One bedroom, Lily. Alone on the bed. Unharmed.

Their eyes locked.

"I'm alone," she said. "He left."

Her voice trembled, but she wasn't crying. There was no visible blood spatter on her. He opened the closet and finished checking the room. She was, as she'd said, alone.

"Are you really okay?" He sat on the bed next to her, beginning to gauge her mental state. Her spine was straight. She was shaken but in control. Her skin smelled like Lily's own sweet scent, not gunpowder, not fear.

Praise for Cindy Harrison

Cindy Harrison's heartfelt writings push past the boundaries of the modern romance novel. With humor, honesty, and insight, Harrison tackles a variety of relationship issues. Her books are a delight to read, with well-crafted characters and plots that are sure to keep readers turning the pages.

~ Cindy LaFerle, author of Writing Home

Dedication

This book, as every novel we've worked together on, owes much to my fabulous editor, Eilidh. Thank you for making me better than my best. I also thank my longtime critique group, Bob Baker, Vernie Dale and Tom Phillips, for their intelligence, honesty, and friendship.

Author Note

I have lived in Metro Detroit all my life. A broad generalization is that the suburbs are mostly white and the city is mostly black, although plenty of black people live in the suburbs and a growing number of white people live in the city. The racial divide is real. Racism is alive and thriving. So who am I, a white woman from the suburbs who comes to Detroit on weekends for concerts, plays, and poetry readings, to write a book set in this city?

I've always loved Detroit. It's been the cool place to hang out since Plum Street in the 1960s. I also graduated college in Detroit. Marygrove was once the Catholic sister college to University of Detroit, but by the time I got there, most of the nuns were gone, and the student population was predominantly black. For once, I was in the minority.

It was an eye-opening experience, particularly the things I learned about African American culture, not even most of it from books. In this book, I didn't set out to talk about race relations in Detroit, but as I went on in the story, I realized it had to be there. I did the best I could with what I knew about black people from my intense experiences at Marygrove, which were overwhelmingly positive.

The other thing about Detroit that locals will recognize are the street names, the many neighborhoods within the city, the landmark buildings, the riverfront. Most of the time I used these settings as they are, but, at times, for the convenience of my story, I moved things around a bit. I changed some place names.

Setting aside, this novel is a work of fiction, and none of the characters depicted are real people, living or dead.

~ *CH*

Chapter 1

Lily

I used to have a different name, a different life. Every day in Detroit, I lost another inch of my old identity and didn't miss it. It came back one night while I worked a routine case, staking out a woman from my SUV on a sweaty summer night. My video recorder rolled film as Roseann Heyl, accused adulteress, rang the front bell of the condo building where her supposed lover lived. I filmed Roseann waiting for him to buzz her inside. I was hoping they'd kiss before they disappeared into his condo.

Then I panned to Roseann's stalker. The stalker puzzled me, but my client, Jimmy Heyl, Roseann's husband, had been strangely unconcerned about that weird twist in the case. The stalker was very good. Roseann didn't appear to ever guess she was being followed. When I told Jimmy about Roseann's stalker, he would only say, "I'm paying you to videotape her screwing, not be her damn bodyguard." He had a point. Still, I couldn't help but move my camera back and forth between Roseann and the stalker. Where she went, he followed. There had to be a reason, but I'd tried pressing Jimmy for details and he told me to forget the stalker; he wanted a different film. I figured maybe Jimmy had two PIs working the case. Maybe that's how these things were done in Grosse Pointe, the high-class enclave where Jimmy and Roseann lived.

I wondered if I'd be able to get incriminating videotape tonight. So far, I had a collection of film where nothing happened. Nothing had happened when Roseann met Thomas Kennedy after work for drinks. Nothing happened, not a kiss or caress, when they chose a cozy spot in Greektown for dinner. Nothing for sure happened at her book club, an all-female gathering where Kennedy never appeared, although the stalker did.

At least two minutes had passed since I'd parked and started recording. If Thomas Kennedy was my boyfriend, I'd be pissed because he'd kept me waiting, but it was hard to tell Roseann's mood from this distance. She wasn't tapping her foot or hitting the buzzer again. She just stood there, and probably six feet behind her, just in front of a stand of leafy trees, her stalker stood there too.

While taping this nothing scene, I puzzled out a way to get inside the Flatiron Building and into Thomas's condo for the money shot I'd been hired to record. I'd scanned the windows when I'd arrived a few minutes ago, and only three of the units had open blinds. I'd gotten my hands on an owner's directory a few days ago and knew which unit was Kennedy's. His blinds weren't open. I wasn't willing to do anything illegal like break into the building and then somehow steal into Kennedy's apartment. Unfortunately, these two did not frequent the kind of sleazy hotels whose gaping drapes allowed me, from a discreet distance, to film people caught in the act.

I decided somewhere in the third minute of filming

that I was done with this type of case. Missing persons and insurance fraud only from now on. In the still sweaty night, a rustle of wind went through the trees, bringing me back to what I was filming. The stalker had raised a gun, elongated by a silencer, and I caught the flame from the shot, like a kitchen match striking in the dark.

The sound had not been entirely suppressed. What I'd mistaken for trees rustling in a stray breeze had been the weapon discharging. Horrified, I quickly panned to Roseann and saw her body hit the ground. I popped open the glove box and got out my Sig, but by the time I'd climbed out of the car and started running toward Roseann, the stalker was gone. Weapon in hand, I rushed to Roseann's side. I smelled blood before I saw it pooling around her hair. My eyes swept the trees. He was gone. I tucked the Sig into the waistband of my jean shorts, then dialed 9-1-1. I put the phone on speaker and set it down on the brick pavers as the emergency operator explained in a calm voice how to check for a pulse. I knelt beside Roseann and did as instructed. The skin on Roseann's neck behind her ear was smooth, still warm.

That was the moment I remembered kneeling down to another dead body, in another life, checking for a pulse, feeling nothing but still warm skin. It had been summer then, too.

"No pulse," I told the operator, whisking my fingers away just before the panic started. The episodes feel like I'm under flashing lights, then everything fades into fog. My doctor calls it a fugue state. I'm not sure which is worse, a terrifying attack of sheer panic or going into the know-nothing fog.

I'm not sure how I got back to my car. One minute I was kneeling next to a dead body, and the next, Detective Derrick Paxton knocked on the passenger side of my window. I came out of the fog, immediately panicked, my entire body jerking in a strong startle reflex. He waited a beat while I tried to collect all my flying parts with deep breaths.

I'm in PTSD recovery. I hadn't had a panic attack or popped a sedative for a couple of months, not since that first time I met Paxton. It must have been the position I'd been in tonight, kneeling over Roseann's dead body, that triggered everything.

"Lily." Paxton put a period after my name. I kept up the deep breathing as uniforms and EMS, an entire awful circus, rolled past us. I unlocked the passenger door, and Paxton slid in. "Who you working for?"

I took a breath. Then another. I held out my hand to show Paxton it was steady. I'd had to go through my PTSD story with him last time we'd met. He didn't look impressed with my supposed calm, just waited for an answer. Finally, I blurted, "What about client privilege?"

He didn't say anything, just waited for me to do the right thing. That got me more than if he'd insisted I tell him everything immediately.

"Jimmy Heyl," I admitted. Paxton would have heard of him. Jimmy was a big deal around town. Businessman with his own investment firm. Friend to public television and local charities. Supporter of the opera house and season-ticket holder to private boxes for viewing local sports teams. Paxton didn't ask anything else. I was grateful and surprised that he didn't request my video recorder. What had I done with it?

Ah, right, I'd dropped it into the glove box when I'd pulled out my gun. I started to feel distant from myself, like looking out the wrong end of a telescope, but I pressed my hips into the back of my seat and felt the security of a warm gun. Even as I tried for composure, I struggled with the anger I felt about this relapse. I needed to give myself a break. After all, it had been a while since I'd seen a dead person.

Paxton asked if I'd witnessed the shooting, and I said yes. I showed him the direction where I'd seen the stalker. I admitted I hadn't seen which way he'd run. "He just sort of melted into the trees," I said.

From what seemed like a long way away, I heard him say, "I'll be tied up for a while here, but I'll need a full statement."

"Can we talk at my place instead of me coming down to the station?" I must have looked as bad as I felt, because he nodded, then got out of my car and went to do his job. I started the engine, and while I had had every intention of heading home when I said so to Paxton, driving calmed me. So I went to Corktown instead.

****

One thing I like about Detroit is it has neighborhoods. Famous ones like Greektown and Indian Village, but smaller ones too, like the Irish-infused Corktown. Jimmy's girlfriend, Abby, was the barkeep at the Old Shamrock, so I checked there first. Yes, Jimmy cheats, was cheating well before he suspected Roseann of doing the same. It's a dirty, double-standard world.

The place was quiet, empty but for the two of them, this not being St. Patrick's Day and fake Irishmen in short supply.

"I'm very sorry, but—" I didn't know how to tell someone his spouse was dead. I looked at Abby standing there. Should she hear this? "Bad news," I finally said.

"Can we get a little privacy, Abby?" Jimmy wasn't really asking. Abby vanished into the kitchen just off the bar. We had the room to ourselves. After I told him as gently as possible that Roseann had been murdered, Jimmy went behind the bar and poured himself a vodka. Neat.

"Been here long?" I had to ask. The whole stalker thing was falling into a new category for me, but I owed it to my client to figure out if he'd hired the hit man, or if maybe he was the stalker himself.

"Only all night." He poured another shot into his rocks glass, again omitting the rocks, and came out from behind the bar.

"Anybody else, other than Abby, in here tonight?"

"Yeah." Jimmy was a handsome guy, mid-forties, startling blue eyes, full head of dark hair. Right now, he looked stunned.

"Who, Jimmy? Who else was here?"

"Everybody." He glanced around the empty room, biceps bunching under his shirt. His blank face slowly rotated back to me. "Let me think." He drank the vodka and sat back down. "Abby," he yelled. When she came back in, it was clear from the way her eyes bugged out that she'd heard everything. "Give Ms. White here the names."

"Names?" Abby said, acting as if she hadn't heard a thing.

Jimmy just looked at her.

"Sorry, Jimmy," she said, lowering her eyelids. She had just turned to speak to me when Paxton walked in. Clever Jimmy sent me a quick text before the detective was fully in the door. I saw him type it, heard my phone ping. Jimmy gave me a look full of significance, but I didn't know what it meant. I'd read his text later.

Paxton, an immaculate dresser who wore well-cut suits with elegant ties like tonight's baby blue and navy pinstripe, pushed away the peanut shells that littered the floor with his highly buffed leather shoes. I wondered if he resisted an impulse to shake his foot loose from the debris. He flashed his badge at Jimmy. "You can go now, White." He didn't even spare me a glance, but his voice said he was pissed. "Go home this time."

"Should I call your lawyer?" I said to Jimmy, glancing at Paxton.

"No," they both answered.

Paxton wanted me out of the equation, and Jimmy thought his alibi was solid. Paxton would just have to get used to me sticking to my client until the job was done, and Jimmy's confidence about not needing a lawyer made me feel he probably wasn't the stalker-shooter. So did he hire a hit man or not? Maybe his text would tell me something.

I got in my SUV and checked the text from Jimmy. The time came up first. Close to closing time, which is two a.m. in Detroit. I touched the text app.

FIND STALKER

All caps. Jimmy took time to lock those caps in. The significance of his last look at me was now clear. He wanted me on the case in a totally different capacity. My hands wanted to tremble on the wheel of the SUV, but I wouldn't let fear consume me. I wanted to find the shadow man who'd murdered Roseann. I wanted to know why he'd done it, who'd hired him. I wanted to know if Roseann and Kennedy were really having an affair. After that, not before, I could close the case.

Worst thing that could happen? I suppose I could get myself killed, but I was half-dead already. I'd attempted a resurrection of sorts when I'd left my old life behind, but it hadn't worked. Not fully. Not if a murder could put me back in the grip of a panic I couldn't claw my way out of, like one of those nightmares where you're trying to move away from the monster but you're paralyzed. I spent several years dealing therapeutically with that panic. Back then, when I was in the grips of a panic so strong I thought it would stop my heart, sometimes I wished it would. But I'm better now. I have to be. With a panic attack, you only *feel* like you're dying. But I'm still alive. For now. And my job depends on me staying that way.

I didn't kid myself about my job being so special. Sometimes I found men who skipped out on child support. Sometimes I caught people cheating the system with false medical claims. It might be tiny compared to what Paxton did, but everyone needs a purpose, and mine was a grim determination to not let the bad guys win. This type of job came naturally to me. There'd been two bad guys in my past—one was in the grave and the other in prison. And I'd put them both there.

As usual, when even a hint of the past comes to mind, I pushed it away and thought about the current situation. Two things occurred to me: one, Jimmy was innocent. Two, he was guilty, but he thought sending me that text would convince the stupid girl detective of his innocence. Either way, I'd show him Lily White was made of stronger stuff.

As I tooled up Woodward Avenue, images from tonight's video unreeled in my head. My hands jumped on the wheel. Nervous tension traveled up my arms and into my neck and throat then shot down to my stomach. I needed a pill. I quickly pulled into the parking garage of the Iroquois Casino, the place that held the suite I called home these days. It sounds weird, living in a casino, but I feel safe here. I'm convinced my mother would say I was putting her money to good use. She would know this casino was my friendly neighborhood and my refuge. It's also where I met Paxton for the first time. But that's another story.

Once inside my room atop the casino, I popped a tab of anxiety medication, called room service, and ran a bath. As I soaked, I mentally filed through the dozens of cases I'd worked since obtaining my PI license. None had come to such deadly conclusions as the tragedy tonight, but I'd seen assault and witnessed domestic abuse more than once. There had been a knife fight early on, which made me believe some of the negative hype about the city. The knife incident triggered a strobe, and before I fogged out, I'd run down the street and into the Iroquois, where I reported the crime to the desk clerk and asked for a room in the same breath. Not that I was stupid enough to believe a hotel lock would keep me safe if someone wanted to do me harm, but I'd needed an immediate bolt hole and later found it suited me.

For example, tonight the soaking tub was perfect, the clean towels thick and warm, and the lavender spa products smelled nice. Lavender was supposed to relax.

I let the bubbles and the meds do their work until I heard room service knock.

I folded myself into the thick robe I grabbed from a hook in the bathroom. The robe covered me pretty much from head to toe, so I padded across the bedroom to the living area, opened the door, and allowed the waiter to roll in my dinner. He set everything on the little dining table next to the window. The window showed city lights still sparkling in the predawn sky. Nice view. It wasn't half so pretty in daylight.

The kitchen had layered fresh turkey and cheese on a toasted pretzel roll, with the exact amount of mayo I liked. They'd included a half bottle of Pinot Noir with the meal. I wasn't hungry, but I hadn't eaten all day and I wanted that wine. I tipped the waiter and closed the door behind him. Then, still in my robe, I ate with one hand while I copied the video to a thumb drive in hope Paxton wouldn't take my camera if I gave him the jump drive instead. I added the video to my external hard drive as extra insurance.

I knew Paxton would arrive soon, or he'd send one of his junior detectives, so after eating half my sandwich, I threw on jeans and a fresh top while I sipped the second glass of Pinot. I thought about popping another chill pill, but the first one plus the wine had dialed me down a few notches, and I didn't want to get dependent on benzos again. Also, I preferred not to be too relaxed when I talked to Paxton. I had to tell him about the stalking. I had to recount everything that had happened on this case so far, and then I had to be willing to hand over my camera. Maybe even my Sig.

He showed up an hour or so after I'd seen him in

Corktown, double coffee shot in hand.

"Alibi hold up?" I handed him the thumb drive.

He didn't ask what it was—just stuck it in his pocket. He nodded in answer to my question. "For now," he said.

Then I told him everything. He took my camera and the Sig. Fine. I had a couple more firearms in a lockbox and more video equipment than a PI really needs. I was a videographer in my former failed attempt at an adult life. It's not as long a stretch as you might think from videographer to PI. Paxton let me keep my phone, something I hadn't even considered losing until he'd demanded to see the text Jimmy had sent me.

"Video show anything?" He wanted my take, which surprised me. I knew the film would reveal everything I could share and maybe more when he pored over it later with the crime technicians.

"Not much more than I told you." I'd gone over every detail, but I had to give him something else. I felt like I owed it to him. He hadn't said a word about me not revealing all this earlier, at the crime scene. "He's an excellent marksman."

"So sure it's a he?"

"Posture, build, body frame, gait...all suggest a male shooter."

"Why didn't Heyl care about the stalker?"

I told him my initial theory about two PIs. Then I told him I'd been worried it was Jimmy until he'd texted me. "Jimmy gets what he wants. Maybe he just wanted a different set of pictures."

"Of her with Kennedy."

I nodded. "The Flatiron is like a fortress. Shuttered tight. And Kennedy never buzzed her in, never came down to the lobby."

"You were in bad shape at the scene."

Understatement. I'd been in no shape at all to be questioned, and I guess he knew it, because he decided to fill in a few blanks for me.

"We got lucky with Kennedy. He came down while we were still at the scene. You were there. In your car." Paxton stopped for a minute to look me over. He'd never shown any interest in me besides concern. He'd never been anything but kind. He looked at me, yes, but it was in a way that made me feel he wasn't just looking, but looking out for me.

"Kennedy told us Roseann was his co-worker. Said he wasn't sure why she'd shown up at his place. He hadn't been expecting her. I put the pieces together, knowing sometimes a PI will still catch a cheating spouse case, but Kennedy says there's no affair. He was in another unit with a group of people, so he didn't hear her buzz. That checked out."

"Thanks. I really did mean to just go home, but I felt stronger when I started to drive, and, you know how it is, first priority is the client."

"Before yourself? Before the law?"

"Yes and no, but mostly yes."

He huffed, but I bet he put his job first, too. His father was the chief of police. Solving cases was in his blood.

"I never saw Kennedy come down," I said. "That's good to know. Thanks again."

This time I got a more assessing look. But he didn't speak for a few minutes. Nobody said anything; he just sat there with me.

"You okay?" He finally broke the silence, which

had been kind of nice. Peaceful, even.

Paxton knew what had happened to me tonight. The strobes, the fugue, the panic. And I knew that was why he hadn't hauled me down to the precinct for a statement the minute he saw me in Corktown. He'd interviewed me after the knifing the first night I'd stayed here at the casino, seen me in the grip of panic and fear and dread. Once I settled down, with the help of my friendly blue pills, I'd explained the whole thing to him, about the PTSD, how I was now recovered, mostly. How I'd originally fallen into the disorder, and how it had worsened as events in my former life continued to spiral out of control. That's when he remembered me from the long-ago video that had gone viral on YouTube, the video where I got my dad to confess to killing my mom.

Chapter 2

Paxton

Paxton left the Iroquois casino less than pleased with how his case had begun. He had allowed a witness to leave the scene, he hadn't known she'd videotaped the murder, and perhaps worst of all, she'd taken it upon herself to inform the victim's next-of-kin. Paxton could never get back those first few moments when Jimmy Heyl heard his wife had been shot and killed. What Heyl's face, eyes, and body language had revealed were lost to him. Why was Lily White able to veer him so far off his usual efficient track?

He slid into his unmarked vehicle and texted his standard coffee order as he pointed the car toward headquarters. He hadn't seen the inside of his riverfront condo last night. This case was hot, the information and evidence were flowing, and he had to get on top of it now. He'd work the usual overtime when he got a new case and get the jump before the next homicide popped up and demanded his attention. He blamed himself. He'd been too easy on a woman in distress. He knew better. He'd been a cop all his adult life; his dad was top cop in the city; he had uncles and cousins on the force.

On the other hand, thanks to Lily White, he had superior videotape of the crime and the shooter, something he knew was not available in any cameras that might or might not be functional at any location near the Flatiron. Plus he had the added information, and videotaped evidence, that the victim had a stalker. He'd also learned from Lily that Heyl knew about the stalker and had done nothing. It seemed like a slam dunk. Husband guilty. Finding the hit man should be so easy. He needed the state police lab to enhance the video images he'd taken as evidence. There had been something from his first view at Lily's place, some distant bell ringing in his brain. But the face just wasn't clear enough with Lily's equipment. She didn't have a zillion dollar crime lab, like the state police had set up in Detroit PD headquarters.

First, he needed coffee.

He pulled into his favorite coffee shop; they had his order ready. He asked the barista to add another shot of espresso. He thought of Trevor, his last best partner when they'd both been in uniform. Trevor never made it to detective; after a shoot-out at a drug house on the west side of the city, Trev had never been the same. Crime-scene techs had discovered from the forty bullet casings gathered from the dead bodies and the room, Trevor's bullet had been the one to kill an unarmed pregnant woman. She'd been a junkie in the wrong place at the wrong time, but Paxton couldn't get through to Trev, make him see that it had not been his fault. They were being fired on by a dealer with a semi-automatic and several meth-heads with crappy revolvers and tweaking trigger fingers.

"It was us or them, bro," Paxton had told Trev time and again as they sat late at the Local.

Trev kept drinking bourbon after bourbon until he

was numb enough to go home and sleep without nightmares. Paxton had kept Trev's secret, and that weighed on him. He'd stood by and watched his partner go down a road too many officers knew but didn't disclose. Trev treated his remorse and panic attacks with booze and benzos, not therapy. There's never been an official diagnosis of PTSD because Trev kept the code of silence. Police officers in Detroit needed to be tough. Trev believed he wasn't tough enough, wasn't good enough, and it had ended up killing him.

He reached for the doctored coffee and sipped as he pulled away from the drive-through. He realized now why he had gone easy on Lily tonight. He'd recognized something in her the first time they met. After Trev died, Paxton had taken a course on PTSD the department offered. He'd learned the signs, mostly because he wanted to know what Trev had been up against. If he ever had another partner with the same syndrome, he vowed to do better. Lily was not his partner—she wasn't even a cop—but he'd essentially slotted her into that spot where Trev had been lurking these last five years.

The city was quiet this early dawn as he headed toward the Lodge Freeway. He would be putting all this in his notes, start building a case file. He would have to type all the details of tonight in the report, including his fuck-ups. When your father was the chief of police, and you were dealing daily with the distrust between uniforms and detectives, it was smart not to paint over any glitches in the case. Weighing out the evidence gained, he felt okay—not great, just okay—about his handling of Lily White.

As he slid through the empty streets, he recalled

the first time he'd seen Lily. He'd written up a statement, had a case file on her. He'd pull it and add it to his current case file, but he remembered every minute of that encounter. He pulled into the lot at headquarters and went straight to his office to pull that first file on Lily White.

He steadily sipped his coffee and steadily went over the report from that former crime scene, a scene Lily had been a witness to as well. He read the pages, but Paxton kept two files. The official one in his hand now, and another one, an unwritten one, full of the kinds of impressions and suppositions and gut feelings that didn't belong in an official report. He pulled that from his memory. Putting himself back there, reliving it, would give him a fuller picture of this troubled young woman.

The first time he met Lily had been on a downtown block, razed when the Iroquois development went in and used illegally for football tailgates. The city owned the property and frankly didn't have enough manpower to cover it when one of the sports teams had an early game. Nobody from the burbs parked there after dark.

But daytime in Detroit on game day was different. Locals often set up fake parking lot stations at that little scrubby patch of land, collecting fees of up to thirty dollars per car, fleecing the unwitting suburbanites. Sometimes, like today, disagreement over territory led to an altercation between two enterprising young men, both of whom were setting up their phony collection stations complete with ropes to keep out cars that didn't pay. These ropes were haphazardly anchored with cement blocks. By the time Paxton arrived at the scene just after two uniforms, the cement blocks were slick with blood from the knife fight, as were the few vehicles already parked in the lot. The daytrippers were giving statements to one uniform while another had already cuffed the two suspects, who were beat up and bloody but not dead.

Paxton had quickly surmised this was not homicide, not his case. Nobody was dead. At least not yet. An ambulance came roaring to the scene while more uniforms from a second squad car emerged to manage the gathering crowd and to collect evidence. Things were under control, but Paxton had checked with the first responders out of courtesy. "Anything I can do here?"

"One guy was stabbed in the groin pretty bad, but the rest are outer slices. Amateurs."

"The guy with the artery bleed gonna live?"

"Debatable. It was pumping out pretty good, we slapped white on red, applied pressure, and now EMT has it."

"Okay. Anything else?"

"One of the witnesses—a white woman, alone, not a working girl by the look of her—fled the scene." The uniform had pointed toward the Iroquois casino and hotel complex.

"I'll track her down," Paxton said. "Get a statement."

The uniform just nodded. There was a reason beat cops didn't like detectives much. They did the dirty work, first responders, handling crime scenes, interrogating witnesses, writing initial reports. They only handed off the cases after the grunt work had been done, and they resented it. Detectives for the most part resented that the uniforms didn't show the respect their superior rank deserved. Paxton didn't let that shit bother him, and he helped out when he could, just as he had tracked Lily White to the Iroquois that day.

She'd already booked a suite when he found her. She made him show his badge before she let him into the rooms. He knew almost right away what he was seeing as she opened the door was a replay of Trevor's panic attacks. The ones he would never admit to. The ones he treated with booze and drugs, not therapy. She was deathly pale, even for a white woman with fair skin. Her hands shook uncontrollably as she held the door for him. Her body movements were jerky, and her eyes jumped around.

"I—I—he was going to kill her!"

Oh, Christ. She wasn't having a panic attack. She was having a flashback. Paxton winced at the thought that he'd learned what to do to help someone with PTSD far too late to save Trev. One night, his last good partner had climbed into his bathtub, put his service revolver in his mouth, and pulled the trigger.

"Ma'am, what's your name?" He'd already taken a photo of her name on the hotel's registration book, but it was illegible. The Iroquois didn't inquire too closely into the particulars when people with cash wanted rooms. They hadn't gotten her license number.

She seemed to come out of it, whatever scenario she'd been flashing back to. "Lily. Lily White."

"Lily, can I see your ID?"

She jerked so much it was difficult for her to open her purse. Finally, he helped her unfold her wallet. She was a PI. Odd profession for someone with PTSD.

"Lily, do you have medication?"

"Yeah, yes." She took a bottle out of her purse and

while she struggled with the childproof cap, he got a bottle of water from the sideboard and brought it over to where she sat on the sofa.

She popped her pill, then said, "I don't take these anymore." She tossed the prescription bottle—a popular benzo, he noted—on the sofa between them. "Well, I haven't. Not for over a year. I've been in recovery."

"We deal with PTSD in our line of duty, so I understand you were likely triggered by the event in the parking lot."

"Yeah. It's fine. I'll be fine. I feel safe here."

"Are you up to giving me a statement?" Paxton wondered if he should allow the medication to take effect before he began questioning her. It was the first time he'd used his PTSD training.

He noted her hand holding the bottle of water was steadier.

"The placebo effect," she said and laughed.

He laughed with her, but they both knew PTSD was anything but funny.

"What were you doing in that area?" It wasn't an interrogation, just an interview. He was possibly being too thorough, but he liked to know the PIs working his city streets.

"I've been working a case. Insurance fraud. My guy was at a tailgate, drinking tequila and raising hell at ten a.m. I figured I'd get good footage, as he's supposed to be on crutches with his leg in a brace. I parked in front of the liquor store across the street to avoid the dueling parking-lot scammers. I crossed the road and tried to saunter past inconspicuously. I was using the video function on my phone. You'd be surprised how good those images are.

"The first guy—the lighter-skinned one with the goatee—went from angry words to pulling a knife in seconds. The other guy had a knife too and presto! They were slicing and dicing each other. I started to strobe—that's like my signal that I'm having an episode—and I fled. I'm sorry. I fled the scene. My SUV is still at the liquor store. I came here because…well, it was around the corner and I needed a bolt hole."

Paxton had to give the hot mess of a woman her due. She'd given a coherent, calm, concise statement despite her destabilized mental state. Somewhere early, she had learned resilience. His gut told him it would serve her well.

"Did anyone die?" Lily had asked him.

"Not yet." He'd waited a beat. "You get your footage?"

"I didn't. But I will next time. Meanwhile, I have my eye-witness report."

He could see the medication beginning to work. It was a fast-acting benzo, and it loosened her tongue. She told him about how she'd become a PI as a way to use her degree in videography. How she'd caused a little stir on the Internet with a videotaped confession she'd put up years ago. It had gone viral in days. "I was actually in *People* magazine," she said, with some pride.

Paxton didn't ask if the video was connected to the incident that had sparked her PTSD. She could have come from a stressful background, could have been dealing with issues for years, handling the situations as best she could, until something happened that was the final straw, something really big that brought on full-blown PTSD.

He left Lily, and after filing his witness report, he went home and did a Google search on her. He told himself at the time it was strictly because it was his duty to know every new PI in town. He didn't find her right away. She'd changed her last name. But with just a bit of digging, there it was, the infamous video. Other videos, too, some commissioned from small towns in northern Michigan, some from (she explained in voice-overs) college assignments. Then the news clips came, and he put it all together. "Stressful background" didn't begin to cover it. He thought she was brave and foolish to come to Detroit, a tough city for cops, let alone civilians. And her choice of profession—well, he wasn't sure what people with degrees in videography did these days. Make films? Okay, maybe not such a stretch.

He'd drained his coffee by the time he finished reading the report and remembering the stuff that wasn't in the official record. He hadn't seen or heard from Lily White again after that first interview, hadn't given her another thought, until tonight. He hoped her footage was as good as her reputation claimed. It could help him catch a killer.

He deliberately put both Trev and Lily right out of his mind. He had a case to build. There were a lot of moving parts and good, possibly excellent, evidence already stowed in his black go-bag, and he hadn't even written up a preliminary report. The State Police Crime Lab, in a large area below street level, had been added when the new headquarters opened. He checked roll call on his laptop. Crime lab was currently staffed by one evidence tech, LuAnn LaRue. Paxton liked LuAnn.

He called her on his way up to his office and said he'd be down to see her in ten; he had to file a quick report first. She said she was bored and hoped he had something good.

"I hope so, too, LuAnn." Then he clicked off the phone, jogged two flights down, and entered the open area flanked by cubicles.

He spotted Bill Nigel in the bullpen. Nigel, a uniform with aspirations toward detective, was eager and smart, a stroke of luck for Paxton. Paxton's most recent partner, another loser in a series of unreliable partners, was currently suspended pending IA investigation. Meanwhile, Paxton was working alone. Tonight, he might have caught a break with Lily White's help. With any luck, Nigel would pitch in, too.

Night shift was either heading in or still out on duty. Day shift wasn't due for a few hours. He didn't know Nigel all that well, but he could use an extra pair of hands. He said as much, then gave Nigel the bullet points.

"Sounds like a professional hit," Nigel said.

Paxton agreed with a nod. "Heyl's alibi was solid enough that arrest wasn't an option, but we can bring him in for questioning. His lady friend, too. I'd like you to tail them today until noon or so, and if nothing pops, bring them in for questioning."

"You think he'll change his story?"

"I think he's lying about where he was at the time of the murder, and I think she might be covering for him, so if anybody changes their story, it will be her."

"The guy had a mistress." Nigel went through the probables aloud. "Thought his wife was cheating, too. Hired a PI. When he learned about the stalker, told the

PI not to worry about and not to tape the stalker. That right there."

Paxton agreed. Paying for videotaped proof of cheating despite the no-fault divorce laws, telling a PI specifically not to tape a "nothing-to-worry-about stalker"—these facts were compelling but probably not enough to get a warrant. He'd try anyway. Didn't matter if Heyl had an alibi, not really, not if he hired a pro to do his dirty work for him. In Michigan, the guy who hired the hit man was as much a murderer under the law as the one who pulled the trigger.

"From the footage I viewed, the pro felt familiar. Local. Something in his stance." He couldn't be sure until he got some facial enhancement. The same tools should show particulars of the weapon, too.

"Who's in the crime lab?" Nigel asked.

"LuAnn."

Paxton's text pinged. LuAnn asking for ten minutes.

"LuAnn's polishing her magnifier lenses. Or dusting off her keyboard," Paxton said to Nigel.

Nigel nodded, then asked, "Who's on them in Corktown?"

"McDonald." Paxton opened his laptop and started the preliminary report while Nigel contacted the uniform about to end his shift. Typing out the report didn't take long. He'd embellish it later, but for now it was enough to send up the chain of command.

"You think I can come down to the crime lab with you? McDonald in Corktown says they haven't left the bar. She's got the apartment upstairs, right?"

"Correct. They're likely sleeping or sexing. Sure you can come down to the lab, but relieve McDonald when night shift goes off." If he had any qualms about pulling double duty, Nigel didn't air them. Paxton was liking the guy more and more. "Let's give LuAnn five more minutes."

"Sure. I wanted to ask you about that thing that went down last year, if that's okay," Nigel said. "You know I've put in for homicide detective."

Paxton hadn't, but that was better yet. Nigel would need a trial by fire to get him moved up quickly.

"So the shootout at the precinct—was that why you got the promotion to detective?"

Paxton nodded, gratified someone believed that hard work, not his connections up the ranks, had landed him a private office. Nigel was talking about a precinct attack that had wounded four officers. It had been a year after Trev died, Paxton was still in blue, and it was broad daylight. There were easily eight to ten men, uniformed officers all, milling around the bullpen behind an open space half circle where dispatch sat on the main floor. A lone gunman entered and immediately began spraying the place with his semi-automatic. Cops swirled, diving for cover, then taking shots at the constantly moving assailant, who never stopped dancing, never stopped raining bullets, although he'd been hit several times. He just refused to die until Paxton put him down with a shot to dead center mass that laid him flat. They never knew this lone gunman's motive. There had been no beef with the PD or the precinct. *No dead cops* was good enough to get him his promotion.

That and the fact that he'd taken that damned PTSD course and had gotten recognition for it only because nobody else wanted to do it. Or perhaps because of that. Constant retraining was part of the job, and Paxton had shown he was up for it. He'd shown, according to the official records, "courage in the line of duty."

"Do you think…is there anything I can do to help make rank?"

"Just keep doing what you're doing right now. I'm down a partner, and you can remedy that. This is an unusual case, two murderers. If we collar both of them, that's all good. Do you train?"

Nigel looked perplexed.

"You know, take courses, advance your knowledge and skills?"

"I've got a new baby and a lonely wife, so no."

"Well. Your call, but it helps to show you're willing to work around the clock on cases and still fit in training during your limited down time. Maybe hire a mother's helper for your wife so she can take up a hobby or go to the spa."

Nigel laughed. Paxton knew the guy's salary wouldn't cover anything like that. But then Nigel said, "I could ask my ma to help out. It's for our future, after all."

"Good man," Paxton said, meaning it.

Chapter 3

Lily

I sat in Dr. Cam's office at eight a.m. Saturday morning, feeling guilty for demanding an immediate weekend appointment after not seeing her for months. "Thank you for fitting me in. I know you don't usually see patients on Saturday."

Dr. Cam studied me before answering. "I'm glad you called," she finally said, "in light of your situation."

I had told Dr. Cam about the shooting and my reaction to it over the phone; I knew this must be why she opened her office to me so early and on a weekend.

"So you had an episode. But here you are. You did all the right things. You got a good night's sleep, you called me, you got in your car, you drove to my office. How are you feeling?"

"Emotion or mood?"

"Start with either."

"I'm so angry at myself. I feel guilty. I had a previous episode, and I didn't call you. I thought I could handle it on my own. I thought I had handled it. My mood is dark, but I'm struggling against it."

"What happened with the first new episode? How long ago was it?"

"A couple of months." I told Dr. Cam about the first episode, when the two thugs had sliced each other to bloody messes.

She didn't comment about the time between the two instances. "Okay, well, it's not unusual for people in recovery to have bumps in the road. Each episode would traumatize anyone."

I felt relief flood me. I wasn't a freak. It wasn't a done deal that I was heading back to where I'd been. "I just want to move on," I said.

"Best thing to do," Dr. Cam agreed. "But for now, just let yourself use the medication if you feel unease ramping up to panic out of the blue."

I nodded. "I get anxious when I think about what happened, and I get anxious when I think about what I missed while in that fugue state."

"How much time passed between the murder and the detective knocking on your car window?"

I was an obsessive keeper of time. You have to be when you're a PI. For reports and a million other reasons. "The shooter fired at 12:02 a.m. The detective knocked on my window at 12:09 a.m." Seven minutes. Lost forever.

"You know you armed yourself and went to help the victim. You know you called 9-1-1 and talked to an operator."

"Oh!" I started to relive those moments.

Dr. Cam waited.

"I knelt down. To see if there was a pulse. To see if she was alive."

"Why is that important?"

"It didn't hit me at first, when I was on with the emergency operator, but after, I started to get up, and I flashed back to when I killed my cousin. My body remembered it. I had bent over his body the way I bent over Roseann Heyl's."

"A forceful trigger like that would cause anyone a hiccup. But let's talk about the time in light of this. After the shot was fired, you can account for most of your time. It had to take four or five minutes to kneel, feel for a pulse, put in a call, talk to emergency personnel. Then the muscle memory kicked in, and you simply shut off for a minute or two. You walked to your car, a safe place. You waited there for the detective."

I felt better but also stupid. Why couldn't I have done my own timeline? The fact that I was out of it for even a second loomed so huge. Like a lot of survivors, sometimes I think my symptoms are going to take over my life to the point that I cannot function. "I worry about fugue. I like to be in control. Or at least aware."

"And usually you are. You chose a career that requires hypervigilance."

I nodded.

"So this detective. Quite a coincidence he was there both times."

I shrugged. I explained that I'd interacted with dozens of police officers in the time between the two occasions I'd seen Paxton.

"He remembered you."

"And I remembered him. He's very kind. He makes me feel safe. When I saw him, I snapped right out of the fugue." I felt guilty all over again for not going right home when Paxton told me to. I had inserted myself into his investigation. I hadn't thought of it that way at the time. Still, he'd been cool about it.

We talked some more about my choice of career. Dr. Cam had been skeptical before, and now she was really hinting that maybe I should find something else to do. I had more options than most people.

"I've thought about it. I'm funding a rape crisis center in the city. They asked me to be more involved, like, put a face on the organization. But I don't want to do that. I gave them more money so they could hire someone photogenic and charming with PR savvy."

"What else…?"

"There's nothing else I want to do. I don't want to make documentary films. I don't want to film indie screenplays. I don't want to teach film. I like to film real people in the act of committing real crimes. Just not homicide."

Dr. Cam nodded. We'd been through all of that stuff in so much more detail before.

"It was a mistake to take this case. I don't usually do them; they don't come along so often now that divorce is no-fault. If I stick with missing persons and the insurance fraud cases, I'll be fine."

Dr. Cam did not look convinced, but I'd gotten what I came for. She said that relapse was normal, and that mine had been minimal. I would be fine. I left her office without making another appointment, and she didn't suggest I book one.

Next stop would make me feel even better about my abilities. It's one of those inexplicable paradoxes: guns kill people, but shooting one makes me feel alive.

Chapter 4

Paxton

LuAnn LaRue assessed the footage Paxton had acquired via Lily. "This is not your typical surveillance video," she remarked. "Extreme superior quality." Paxton was grateful for the videography student who decided to become a PI.

He stood over LuAnn's shoulder, Nigel at his side. She used her high-tech tools to enhance the dark images. The automatic weapon and silencer were of the grade and caliber Paxton expected from a professional. The crime scene spatter, chunks of the victim's brain mixed in with the blood, told the story on the type of bullets used. The crime-scene guys had confirmed it.

"The stance of the shooter indicates probable injury of the right knee," LuAnn observed. She pointed out the way the guy wobbled very slightly as he shifted.

"Bingo," Paxton said.

"What?" Nigel said.

"Not what. Who. LuAnn can you get his face any clearer?"

She shot up the resolution, and there was the face, the long black braid barely visible at night.

He nodded his thanks. "Send these resolutions to me? Keep at it, and send everything else you find."

"I'm off the clock in less than an hour."

"So then we're good." Paxton knew she'd work that film until she'd discovered the brand of the shooter's socks.

Paxton left the tech, and Nigel followed.

"You know the guy?" Nigel asked.

"Yeah, I'm thinking he's local. Indian, goes by the name of Bingo." Paxton shook his head to indicate his disdain for the nickname. "The timeline from the PI surveillance is interesting. Why would Bingo follow Roseann Heyl for days before executing the job?"

"Interesting," Nigel remarked.

"I can give you the case file to read, but quick summary, Bingo has been in prison for the last few years. He shot some guy in the foot at a bar in Grosse Pointe. Claimed it was justice, as the guy had shot him in the knee the month before. Unfortunately for Bingo, his victim lost a leg due to infection, and Bingo got sent away with his bum knee. Looks like prison rehab is subpar." Paxton allowed himself a grim smile. That shooting in Grosse Pointe had not been his case. It was out of city limits. He'd read about it all online, including the stupid knee-revenge motive.

"Word on the street was he'd been target practicing for a month before that night at the bar. I bet he's been practicing more since he got out, what, six months ago now. And he's setting up shop here in Detroit, an excellent place for a newly minted hit man to find a client."

"What do they do? Advertise?" Nigel asked.

"It's all online now, most of the time. Dark sites. We'll need IT to look into that. They can work from one end, the guy who hired Bingo, main suspect Jimmy Heyl. I can call tribal police for a recent address on

Bingo. That happens, and I'll apply for a warrant so we get his laptop and firearms. Bing, bang, boom."

"If he's still here," Nigel said.

The man had a point. Paxton thought they'd get along just fine.

Who's your PI?" Nigel asked.

"Lily White. We've crossed paths before. She's okay. What I'm thinking is, if Bingo's going to fly out of City or Metro, like any pro worth his fee would do after completing the job, maybe we can nail him before he gets on a plane."

"You want me to track that down?"

"I'll do that. You stick with Heyl. With any luck, we'll have two busts in less than twenty-four hours."

Chapter 5

Lily

After a mostly sleepless night going over and over my footage of Roseann and not finding anything new or enlightening, I jammed the key into my gun box. I had not opened it since I began my new life two years ago. I'd wanted a new gun to go with the new life, so I'd purchased the Sig. I lifted the lid of the box and looked at the girl-colored gun I'd bought on a whim. Pink had never really been a comfortable fit. So instead of the silly pink gun, I chose my Kimber, an old friend, a custom 9mm with a gorgeous rosewood grip. It was the gun I'd learned to shoot with, the gun I'd used to kill my cousin. I hadn't taken it out of the lock box since the police had returned it, having ruled that death of the evil cousin as justifiable homicide.

I lifted the Kimber from the box. It slid into my purse like it was home. I went to the Sportsman's Club for target practice. Target practice was a good idea for a PI in Detroit. It was also aversion therapy. One way to supposedly "cure" PTSD is to systematically recreate the circumstances that caused it. Since I couldn't go get myself raped by a relative every day, I re-enacted killing the creep. I'd sound remorseful if he hadn't been about to rape another girl, this one at knife point. If he hadn't laughed when he saw me with my Kimber and pressed the knife harder into her neck, drawing blood.

The Detroit Sportsman's Club was a venerable institution on Jefferson Avenue. It was where I'd met or had referrals from members to many of my clients. The local gun enthusiasts were attracted to my superior ability, honed over long years of schooling. The place reeked of old money, which was not something you'd necessarily think of when you pondered guns. Or Detroit. I'd grown up with newish money, and my gun was my best friend, so I fit in okay.

I had already fired off my usual couple dozen rounds when Jimmy Heyl found my lane.

"Hey," he said.

"You next?" I asked.

"No. Looking for you. You done?"

I nodded and followed him out of the shooting gallery and into a large room, essentially a lobby with pricey rugs and highly polished furniture from another century. We didn't sit.

"So. Find him?"

It had been less than twenty-four hours since the stalker had shot Jimmy's wife. It was still fairly early on a Saturday morning. No, I said, I hadn't found him yet.

"Did you talk to Thomas Kennedy?"

"No. But I'm on my way to see him. The police have my gun. I haven't used the Kimber in a while. Had to practice first."

Jimmy, mollified, asked how it had gone. He didn't ask to see my gun. With these men, that was considered rude. There was an actual rule on the books that, unless you were in your lane, guns had to be holstered at all times. I had a custom holster sewn into all my purses, not exactly the letter of the law, but it worked here.

"Let me know when you get him," Jimmy said.

I nodded, then asked, "How are you?" He seemed to have forgotten he was a recent widower, but I hadn't.

"You know. Roseann's dead. The kids are all flying in for the funeral. I'm the top suspect as far as your Detective Paxton's concerned, so I'm peachy. Just find that guy, White."

Paxton wasn't "my" detective, but I simply nodded. "Just one more question," I said. "Why weren't you concerned about the stalker when I first told you about him?"

Jimmy ran his hand over his eyes and down his face. "I don't know. I was focused on getting the pictures of the two of them. I get like that, where I home in, you know?"

"Yeah," I said, not really feeling that explanation but letting it rest for now. "I'll be in touch." Once I was back in my vehicle and on the road, I hit the control panel to bring up my phone, touching in Thomas Kennedy's number.

"Hi, Thomas. This is Lily White. I'm so very sorry about Roseann."

"I'm sorry—I mean, thank you—but who are you? Do I know you? Did you know Roseann?"

"In a way." I gave him the short version. I didn't want to go into an interview situation with Kennedy based on lies. It felt wrong on so many levels. "So I just wondered if I could stop by and get your perspective on a few things." I had found one picture from early days when I went to Victory Motors headquarters in the Renaissance Center and got lucky at the coffee bar. Roseann had been there with Kennedy plus another man and woman. I didn't know who they were. Kennedy could identify them for me.

"You were the last person to see Roseann alive," he said, a catch in his voice.

"I was. And again, I'm so very sorry for your loss."

"I don't know what I can tell you. We weren't lovers; we had a work project. I already told the police that."

"I know Detective Paxton. He said you had an alibi, but nothing about the work project."

"It was a confidential project." His tone lowered as if his condo might be bugged.

"Would it be okay for me to stop by? I want to find out who killed Roseann. It's my job, but I need to do it for myself, for personal reasons." I wasn't trying to manipulate the guy. I felt dirty, videotaping a murder. The only way I could vindicate myself was to find the killer. Whatever it took. And right now, Kennedy was my best lead.

Kennedy hesitated but then reluctantly said okay.

I stopped at a bakery for muffins on the way to the Flatiron. I'm not normally your warm and fuzzy type, but you have to be somewhat charming when you interview people or they won't open up. So the muffins were my way to sweeten Kennedy. Plus I'd had coffee but no food before practice.

I parked and walked to what had, until an hour ago, been a crime scene. I hit Kennedy's bell as I'd seen Roseann do last night, and he buzzed me in. When I knocked, he opened his door a crack. I flashed my license. "It's Lily White. We just spoke on the phone. It's okay to let me in. I wasn't followed."

"You look too young to be a private investigator.

Can you even shoot a gun?"

I nodded, standing outside his door with my bag of muffins.

He opened the door wide, and I eased in, handing Kennedy the bag of muffins. He peered inside. He smiled, and it changed his face from seriously worried to slightly thrilled. "How sweet. Thank you."

My gut had been saying for a while now that he and Roseann were not lovers. Now I added the feeling that Thomas Kennedy was not a guy who would lie to the police. Something about his face or his voice. He didn't seem versed in lies or smooth talk. His thick glasses and the kind of bedhead, not artfully arranged but smashed up over one ear, made him look like a sweet puppy.

As we walked through his foyer and living space into the kitchen, the open blinds filled the room with light. Kennedy had three computers in his main room, no television. One desktop and two laptops, both closed. The electronics were plugged into the immaculate white walls, but no wires showed. Kennedy had threaded every unsightly cord through white PVC pipe. His desk was glass, the leather chair black, same as the sofa, both devoid of rips or stains. The sofa pillows were lined up like soldiers, and the desk was smudge free. He must have cleaned last night after the police left. I didn't blame him.

The black-and-white theme established in the front living space continued into the kitchen, which featured a black-and-white checkerboard floor. All white countertops, white plates and napkins, which Kennedy efficiently set out for the muffins. White coffee mugs shaped more like bowls and substantial enough to hold dinner had black letters spelling out the word coffee. He poured two cups, black, and motioned me to a seat at the snack bar.

He waited until he'd polished off his first muffin, blueberry—mine was a tart lemon with a sweet glaze on top—before saying, "I'm not sure how I can help you."

"You could tell me about the project you and Roseann were working on." I decided to keep the print I'd run of that image from the RenCen coffee shop in my pocket for a while.

"Oh."

Sometimes, despite my training and constant feedback on my attitude, I was still a little bit impolite. Or I rushed things. I was working on it. "I'm thinking it might have something to do with Roseann's death. Anything that sensitive?"

"Well…it was pretty James Bond."

I sat up straighter, wiped the crumbs off my hands with the napkin he'd provided, and pulled my phone out of my pocket. The phone with the photo. I'd show it to him, but first I wanted to hear a spy story. "Okay if I record this, Thomas?" I took a breath. "I just want to get it right. For Roseann." I took a sip of coffee. Sublime.

"You can call me Tom. And go ahead. It's bound to get out soon anyway." He took a deep breath and brought a second muffin to his mouth. Then he put it back down on the dish. "Here's the thing. You remember when that film company got hacked, and it turned out to be terrorists upset about that movie making fun of Muslims? Since then, it's been happening all the time to corporations, banks, the government."

I nodded.

"Well, somebody is hacking into Victory Motors' mainframe using, from what we can figure, that hack method. Or at least they planted a virus. It just hadn't had time to work before Roseann and I found it."

Terrorists? In Detroit?

"I can see what you're thinking. Why kick a town when it's down? But if Detroit became a black hole, the effect would not just be on the auto industry or on the city. It wouldn't just be on the state. It would affect the American economy in such a way there would simply be no more middle class. There would be poor people and rich people, and it wouldn't take that long to happen."

I nodded. I remembered the last recession. My family's wealth had insulated me from it, but a lot of kids dropped out of college that year. And the next.

"Does Paxton know this?"

Kennedy shrugged, which I took as a no. "He seemed to think Mr. Heyl killed Roseann, and I kind of agree with him."

"So one thing has nothing to do with the other."

"Exactly. It's up to my superiors to report the attempted hack to the authorities. I could be fired if I breached confidential projects. It's in my contract."

"Well, then, why tell me, Tom?"

Kennedy was in the middle of a bite of muffin, having given in to his carb lust. He chewed thoughtfully. "I don't know," he finally said, lifting his coffee for a sip. "I just wanted someone other than the team to know. And I trust you."

The team. I wondered if the two unidentified

people in the photo were part of the team. I'd find out soon. Meanwhile, I felt a little glow in my chest. I was not used to people trusting me. Especially someone I'd been spying on just last night. Kennedy must have read my expression.

"You didn't try to bullshit me. You gave it to me straight. I appreciate that. Also, I love muffins."

We both smiled, unable to come up with a laugh between us. An innocent woman had died last night. Which reminded me…"Any idea why she showed up last night?"

"No. If I was expecting her, I wouldn't have been at the neighbor's."

"Maybe something to do with your project? Something that couldn't wait?"

He thought for a minute, then shrugged. "He was your client, right? Roseann never talked about her marriage. Some people said she was married to the job, and a few of them called me her work husband. But James—that's his name, I know that much—got it all wrong. There was no physical relationship. Not even like an emotional affair. We worked long hours; we were work friends. That was it."

I had the answer to one of my burning questions, but nothing helpful as far as the stalker went. In order to get more, I had to tell more. So I laid out my reasoning for him. "Detective Paxton believes Jimmy still has me on the case because I'm a rookie PI he can hoodwink into believing he is innocent. But there's more to it. Jimmy knows who I really am." I had to give it to him straight. "I used to be somebody else. Jimmy knows I'm not easily fooled, and he knows I'm good at what I do." I picked up my phone and scrolled past the Ren

Cen coffee-shop photo. I found my notorious video, the one that had changed the direction of my life, and handed it to Kennedy. He watched. And watched. Even though I'd edited from more than an hour of footage, it was still a long video. Seven minutes and twelve seconds.

I poured myself another coffee from the black carafe and sipped while he watched. After the video, Kennedy whistled and handed me back the phone. I clicked the recorder function on again. "Now three people in Detroit know who I used to be. Paxton is not as impressed as Jimmy because he's got years on me and I did have that videotaped case a little bit wrong. For a minute."

"You could be wrong again."

I didn't bother to say I've had a lot of experience since then. I'd put in ungodly hours to get my license and had been working almost nonstop since. "Yep. That's why I need to eliminate suspects. So far, the cops have three. You, I've crossed off the list. So that leaves two: James Heyl and a good friend of his, who were together last night. They both have alibis, and not just from each other. An entire room of people saw them." I didn't mention that last night both Paxton and I, Paxton more than me, suspected Jimmy could have been Roseann's stalker. I hadn't mentioned the stalker to Kennedy at all—or the obvious possibility that had been nagging at me since talking to Jimmy earlier—that Jimmy had hired the stalker. Bringing all that up to Kennedy would just make things too complex. And maybe, to poor Kennedy, clearly in way over his head, more frightening.

"When I came over here, I was hoping you'd be

able to tell me if you knew of somebody, anybody else, who wanted Roseann dead. Maybe someone at work. Maybe your real girlfriend, jealous of that work wife. Now, from what you've told me, the killer could be just about anyone—a hacker, a terrorist, a government, a nutcase."

I doubted my photo clip would help sort out the work thing, but I was going to show it to Kennedy anyway and then say goodbye. Before I could pull it up on my screen, he said, "Um, not sure this helps, but I think the hacker is someone inside Victory."

"Really? How do you know?"

"There was a signature."

I didn't know what that meant in terms of computer hacking.

"Signatures take a while to work out, but we were getting there."

"So," I said, "could Roseann have found this signature last night? Was it possible she was bringing it to you?"

"Yeah, I guess," Kennedy said, "but why not just call me?"

Good question. She must not have trusted the phone.

"Did you check your email? Maybe she sent you something?"

"No. I checked last night when the police were here."

Okay, still, maybe the hacker was a co-worker, and maybe he was burning the midnight oil, keeping an eye on Roseann, and maybe he knew somehow she had something, so he followed her to Kennedy's, where he killed her. Lot of maybes in there. But it tracked.

If the stalker was the hacker and if the hacker was also Roseann's killer, he had a motive. Victory Motors' downtown headquarters had maybe seven hundred employees. How many were capable of hacking into a tightly secured system?

"I'm still not exactly sure what makes you think it's an inside job," I said.

"The way it was coded, or written into the software. The software incorporates stuff very few Victory employees utilize. It's a company-security thing. They hand off the specific code to us, and it constantly changes so we're continually updating. Like, daily, if not more often. It's a simple but effective security measure."

"And how many people know this coding and updating technique?"

"There are ten of us."

Now there was a photo that would be useful.

Kennedy thought a second, then added, "Some are at the top level and don't really understand code. They couldn't hack into anything more complicated than a steak."

"So with Roseann gone and you cleared, there are eight suspects for the inside job."

"Well, yeah, but Melanie just started maternity leave, and I don't think she's doing any coding or hacking. She needs the insurance and the paycheck." For whatever reason, he pinked up when he talked about this team member.

"Okay. Seven." I noticed an inflection in Kennedy's voice with this new information. And his face flushed just for a second. "Can I have names? Possible motives?" I pulled out my phone to show him the photo. I didn't want to freak him out, or lose the rapport I'd built, so I showed him an image that very starkly told the story of what I really do. I take pictures of people when they don't know I'm watching. I kept the phone in my hand, trying to weigh the risks and rewards.

He looked at his watch. "I've got another meeting and I'm running late, but I suppose I can give you a list if it helps find Roseann's killer." He started to write it into his phone but then thought better of it and crossed the room to his desk, where he found actual pen and paper. He'd grabbed the paper out of the print tray and it looked like there was something on it, but Kennedy didn't seem to notice.

I'd point it out to him once I got the list, then I'd show him the photo and ask if he'd identify the two unknowns. If they matched anyone on the list.

He was halfway back to the snack bar when the big front window shattered, and he fell to the floor. I tried to deny the pattern of blood and brain spatter from Kennedy's body oozing red on the black and white floor. I tried to deny the sick, sweet, heavy smell of death.

Chapter 6

Paxton

Paxton's phone rang at the same time a text pinged. He heard them through thick layers of sleep. He came awake with the thought that he needed one more fact, one more piece of proof, to get a warrant to search Heyl's bank records and seize his computer. He and Nigel had interrogated Jimmy and Abby for several hours the day before, and neither of them moved an inch from their story. He'd worked thirty hours straight and headed home this morning without that crucial piece of evidence that would get him a warrant. He'd fallen straight into bed and slept so hard his head was a brick on his pillow.

With eyes closed, moving only his arm, he grabbed his phone off the nightstand. Opened one eye to peer at the screen. Abby. His eyes opened fully, and he sat up, throwing his legs over the bed.

"Paxton," he said. He moved, phone in hand, from the bedroom and down the curved staircase, ignoring the bannister, intent on the coffee brewing in his kitchen.

"Hi. I…I want to change my statement."

The machine he'd set last night was still spewing. Almost done. He reached for the cup at the final spurt of steam.

"We can do that." He kept his tone level, took a second to savor that first sip. Something was about to break, he could feel it, but he needed to keep Abby calm and ready to talk. His phone went off again. He ignored the second call. He would not let Abby slip from his grasp.

"I won't get in trouble for lying, right?" Abby asked.

"Believe me, you're helping us, and we're grateful." A nonanswer that sounded soothing.

"It's not me. It's Jimmy. He wasn't at the bar when we said he was. I was afraid to tell you the truth with him there."

Jimmy had not been in the same room at the same time with Abby but whatever. In his business, you got used to excuses and lies. "Do you know where he was?" Paxton had a feeling he'd be getting that warrant today.

"No," Abby said.

That was fine. Heyl lied. Good enough.

Paxton told Abby someone would drive her to the station.

"You're not coming?"

"I'll see you there." He disconnected and dialed Nigel.

"What's the story on our lovebirds?" Paxton asked, sipping coffee. They'd had help keeping an eye on Heyl and Abby overnight and into the early hours. Nigel was currently back on duty in an unmarked car in front of Abby's bar in Corktown.

"They had a loud argument after they left headquarters yesterday. He took her home to Corktown but left shortly thereafter. She's still here."

"Who's on Heyl?" They only had extra uniforms for forty-eight hours. He hoped that would be long enough to nail Roseann Heyl's killer.

"Heyl's family are flying in as we speak. Kids, grandkids. He's been home with the ones who've already arrived." And probably would be at least until the funeral.

"Abby wants to revise her statement." Most likely due to the argument the uniform had witnessed yesterday.

Nigel whistled.

Paxton's phone beeped. Again. He quickly checked. "It's dispatch. Can you bring her in?" Nigel agreed, and Paxton took the call from dispatch while Nigel held. "Jesus," Paxton said, back on with Nigel. "Another homicide at the Flatiron. I'll go; you handle Abby."

Paxton took the staircase up two steps at a time, reading the text. Two words from Lily: *Kennedy's dead.* This had to be the homicide dispatch had reported. But why was Lily there? Again? He didn't text her back. Shooter was at large, she was in danger, and he needed to move.

Ten minutes later, he was out the door. Traffic was light—no baseball game today. Unbelievably, he was first at the scene. Where was the day shift? As much as he wanted to run up those stairs to Lily and the second body, it had fallen to him to secure the perimeter.

A knot of people milled in front of the building. They responded to his terse question. Yes, they were all tenants.

"Somebody else got shot," a woman with purple extensions in her hair said. She pointed up at Kennedy's shattered window.

"Guy came at that window with a cherry picker," said a kid, maybe sixteen, wearing drop-crotch jeans. "He shot off one round, then drove the thing away." The kid used his finger like a pen in the air, drawing a curving line from the street around the corner and behind the building.

Paxton surmised the witness was somebody's child. "What unit are you in?"

The kid gave him a first level number, then added that the cherry picker was lime green.

Sirens. Back up. Good.

Paxton nodded at the uniform who approached, repeated what the young man had said about the cherry picker, then handed the job of further interrogation over to the uniform. He needed to get to Lily. To the body. More uniforms were unrolling yellow crime-scene tape outside the area where the residents had gathered. The uniform next to Paxton was already taking statements.

"I'm going in." The uniform said something, but Paxton didn't catch it. He didn't want to hear that he needed to wait for the scene to be secured, that he needed back up. He took the stairs, two at a time, because standing in an elevator was passive and he needed to be active.

Several unit doors opened a crack on Kennedy's floor; Paxton flashed his badge and told everyone to stay put, officers were on the premises, and would be knocking on doors. Kennedy's door was ajar. *Why?* Paxton drew his weapon and entered the foyer. "Police!" he yelled.

"Paxton, I'm back here," Lily said.

Paxton covered his shoes, taking in Kennedy's

body and the blood, the smell, and the smashed window as he stepped forward. A sheet of bloody paper lay under the victim's hand. Next to the smeared blood, a few typed words. An address. Paxton kept his weapon in one hand, kept his eyes slowly tracking from the blank space in the kitchen to the hallway. With his free hand he reached for his phone, snapped a photo in the general vicinity of the paper.

"You're okay. I'm here now," he called out to her.

He had no idea if she was back there alone or if she was being held hostage. He could see most of the front two rooms, living room and kitchen, from where he stood. He made his way toward the little bit of the kitchen out of view. Nobody. Nobody in the hall either. He stepped deliberately, his weapon ready. Bathroom clear. One bedroom, Lily. Alone on the bed. Unharmed.

Their eyes locked.

"I'm alone," she said. "He left."

Her voice had a tremor, but she wasn't crying. There was no visible blood spatter on her. He opened the closet and finished checking the room. She was, as she'd said, alone.

"Are you really okay?" He sat on the bed next to her, beginning to gauge her mental state. Her spine was straight. She was shaken but in control. Her skin smelled like lotion, not gunpowder, not fear.

"I think so. It…it…"

Her voice hesitated, but her furrowed brow said she was thinking things through, trying to give him an accurate picture. He made his hand light and touched her shoulder just for a second. She didn't flinch, instead released a bit of tension she'd been holding. This was not the Lily of last night, out of it in her vehicle after witnessing Roseann's execution. He gave her time to finish her thought.

"This is horrifying," she finished her sentence.

"Yes," he agreed. "Why were you here, Lily?" A tiny section of his brain insisted he put her into the person-of-interest box, not the trusted-partner category with Trev. Trusted partner was where the bigger section of brain wanted to default. He felt himself resist labeling her a suspect in any of this and made mental note of it, waited patiently for her reply.

"I found a photo. Kennedy and Roseann and two other people. I'd taken it the first day on the case for Heyl. They were having coffee, the four of them, at Victory Motors." She shuddered a breath. "I was going to ask him to ID the other two people in the photo, but I didn't get the chance."

He'd make sure to get that photo from her before he let her go today, but there was time. "How long were you here?"

She checked her phone, held in her hand. Her bag gaped open on the floor next to her. He saw the rosewood grip of a gun. According to her case file, she had four registered firearms.

"Fourteen minutes," she said.

He thought that was a really long time to "not get the chance," but he'd get her full story, a second-by-second breakdown of her visit to Mr. Kennedy, when he took her written statement at the station. "How are you doing?" He'd already asked, already assessed, but he wasn't going to let some kind of subtle symptom or sign of her PTSD escape him. "Do you need a pill?"

"No. I'm fine. Just—ugh. Upset. He was a nice guy. You know?" She winced as if swallowing the bitter facts. "And the other one, the intruder, he didn't see me. I came back here and hid in the bedroom. The intruder did something with the computers—that's what it sounded like. Then he came down the hall to the bathroom. He turned on the water. I thought it was weird, to wash his hands, because if he was a criminal, wouldn't he wear gloves? Then I thought he might be getting a drink of water. But why? You know? *Kill someone, ransack the premises, quench my thirst.* What was his reasoning? Why stop for water?" She took a deep breath. "You know how it is. Anything can mean something at this point."

He nodded. Their jobs had some surface similarities.

"I thought, after he left, while I was waiting for you, he must be on some kind of medication. The kind that makes your mouth super dry. Anyway, that's my big hypothesis of the moment."

Paxton nodded. "You think the same guy who shot Kennedy came up here?"

"I don't know. Maybe the shooter has a partner. Maybe it's a computer-hacking conspiracy." She told him the Victory Motors hacking story Kennedy had shared with her.

Paxton thought about that. No reason Kennedy had needed to tell the police the details of a work problem, but he liked the criminal partner theory because Heyl could be part of it. Bingo shoots the vic, Heyl looks for…what? Information on a computer. An email? A document? An address? Was Heyl as stupid as Bingo and missed the address or had he taken a photo of the address too?

Paxton looked at the address he'd snapped a photo

of. Doctor's office in the West Village. OB/GYN. Could Roseann have been pregnant? He'd know later today, after the autopsy.

"Kennedy had this in his hand." Paxton showed Lily his phone.

She studied it and nodded. "He said a co-worker, Melanie, was pregnant. He wanted me to eliminate her as a suspect. That sheet of paper had been in his print tray. He was going to write a list for me of everyone on the hacking project. I saw there was print on the paper and was going to ask if he needed the info, but then he got shot."

"Okay. You're doing great. So, you didn't get a list. You got one name. First name only. Melanie."

She nodded again, and a sob slipped out before she caught it and slammed her mouth shut. "Oh God. I'm sorry. This is intense. Thank you for coming."

"Lily. You did good." He heard the crime-scene people arriving and eyed the weapon in her purse. "You use that today?"

"Target practice this morning. Then I had it out when the intruder was on the premises. I was standing there." She pointed to the wall between the closet and the door.

"Okay." He took a glove and evidence bag out of his pocket and removed her firearm for a tech to tag. "Hold tight, can you?" The crime-scene people had arrived a few seconds ago. He wanted to know if they'd found the cherry picker. He wanted to know if this was the work of the same lowlife who'd pulled the trigger last night.

They'd already bagged the casing. Same caliber as last night. Best working theory: Bingo hadn't left town.

They'd had people at airport security, but nobody had spotted him. What had been a nagging loose end was now a possible reason. Maybe Bingo's job had only been half done.

"This was in the victim's right hand." A tech showed him the sheet of paper he'd photographed. It was already inside an evidence bag. "Smeared spatter matches probably trajectory of fall."

Paxton nodded. "Saw that. It's an OB/GYN clinic. Not sure why Kennedy had printed it out, but another co-worker, on the same team as him and Roseann Heyl, is apparently pregnant."

The tech looked down the hallway.

"There was an intruder. Witness is in back."

"Intruder? After the shooting?"

"Correct." Paxton thought a minute. Either the intruder had missed the paper under Kennedy's hand or he had photographed it, like he himself had done. There was a third possibility. The intruder was an idiot. That matched Bingo's general description. The guy was a precise killing machine, but he couldn't reason his way out of a paper bag. He'd need a partner to pull this off.

"The witness hid from the intruder in the bedroom. She heard computer sounds and the bathroom tap running water."

The APB on Bingo had been out for nine hours. How did a hit man in a cherry picker divert attention? His mind clicked with the million and one things he needed to do five minutes ago. First, he had to get Lily's statement.

The uniform at the door spoke up. "Folks here want to know when they can come and go again. Tomorrow's Monday. Work won't wait."

Paxton pointed out that this time the crime scene was enclosed. "After you finish with whatever you need outside, plus work in the elevator and on the stairs, people in the lower floors can go about their business. This floor will need to stay clear a little longer." The place had been a crime scene most of the night. Just about the time they'd finished, a fresh killing. And the living still had lives to lead.

Paxton went back to where Lily sat on the bed. She seemed frozen in place. He put his hand on her back and felt the bunched-up muscles under his hand. He gave her what he hoped was a reassuring pat.

"Anybody you need to call?"

"What? Like a lawyer?"

"I was thinking a friend. A doctor."

She sighed, stood, and shook out her shoulders. "I've got a psychological trauma therapist. Dr. Cam. I haven't been keeping regular appointments; I sort of graduated last year. But I saw her this morning."

"Good. Two murders in ten hours is not something you want to sweep under the rug." He wasn't sure why he was so worried about her mental health. Must be that default brain thing again, where he was slotting her into the spot formerly occupied by Trev. It was almost too easy to do. He'd have to guard against it.

"Oh! I wonder if that other woman in the photo I didn't get to show him was pregnant?" She took a photo from her purse and studied it. "Could be. Or not. Her dress has an empire waist, so it's hard to tell." She studied the picture some more. "Maybe." She sighed and sent him an electronic copy of the print photo from her phone. "He really didn't tell you anything about the hack and the virus and it being an inside job?"

"No." Now Paxton wished he'd have waited until they were at the station to start questioning her. He could use a recording for the report.

"He said you kind of were leaning toward Jimmy being the guy who either killed Roseann or hired someone to do it."

Paxton wondered how the hell Kennedy would come to that conclusion.

"It was the questions you asked. And the ones you didn't," Lily said, as if he'd voiced his thoughts. Or she'd read his mind. "You and I are working different clues. In order to exonerate my client, I need to look elsewhere, not at him. I need to look into these murders as maybe being part of the work thing."

Paxton didn't say, in cases like this, nine out of ten times, it was the husband. He didn't say the simplest answer was usually the right answer. Because there was a problem this time, and it went to Lily's point. The OB/GYN address and the pregnant team member. If the intruder had seen that address and connected it to another Victory Motors IT employee, and if the team members were all targets, the pregnant employee could be in danger. Too many ifs, but with enough sway to make him look at Lily in a new light. Her theory was not right, but she was doing right by her client. Too bad he was murder suspect number one.

Chapter 7

Lily

Another dead body, another phone call to Paxton, another interrogation. I held myself together as the crime techs came in and looked me over. They finally ascertained there was no blood on my person, my phone, or my handbag. I stayed steady through the cursory exam. I know how to do that now. It's not that I don't feel; it's more like I can't afford to notice the chill zipping my spine like a dress. Paxton took me out of the Flatiron and drove me to HQ. I didn't resist when he said he had to tape the events of the early afternoon, starting when I knocked on Kennedy's door and ending when Paxton finally appeared.

Headquarters was not downtown, but off the Lodge freeway. "Is this where your office is?" I asked, when we arrived.

"Yes," he said.

I wanted to ask if the chief had an office here too, but he seemed all business as we entered by a side door and whooshed up the elevator to a blank open space in front of cubbies full of voices, ringing phones, and flying paper airplane. Before anyone saw us, Paxton took me down the hall to a room and turned on a television. He read off the time, date, my name, and his.

We went through everything up to Kennedy's

death. Then he got up and left the room. He came back and gave me a water.

"You're doing great. Tell me in as much detail as you can remember what happened after Thomas Kennedy was shot. And if you can, include any relevant thoughts you had along the way. What did you do next?"

"After I reported the shooting, I took a step back from the body. I stood there breathing for a few minutes until I heard a noise near the foyer. I thought you could not have reached the Flatiron yet. Nobody had entered or left the unit since I'd come in with muffins fifteen minutes or so before."

"You checked your watch and said it had been fourteen minutes."

"Right. At the scene. Yes. Okay, so I was not moving. I was waiting for you or someone to come before I moved. Then I felt, I don't know, a chill. And yet, the chill I felt wasn't from the window. It came from a noise like a whisper of a door slowly opening.

"Just as quietly as the intruder entered, I backed down the hall to Kennedy's bedroom. The impeccable creases on the corners of the bed linen broke my heart. I didn't shut the door, too afraid of making a sound. I wanted you to be there, Paxton. But you weren't, and that was my fault. I called you first, instead of 9-1-1. I don't know why."

"That's fine. So did you see the intruder?"

"No. I breathed as quietly as possible and pressed myself against the far wall on the other side of the closet. The intruder would not see me if he glanced down the hallway, although once he poked his head in the room, he wouldn't miss me.

"I pulled the Kimber from the open flap of my purse. The rosewood grip felt like the clasp of a friend. I heard him, out there, in the living area, ignoring the body. So, he's the killer or an accomplice. I took deeper, more deliberate breaths and let my finger find the trigger, just for a moment, then eased off. No sense cramping. I lowered my arm, too, the gun at my side. I hoped I wouldn't have to use it.

"The killer didn't know I was in there. Whatever he was doing in the living area must have to do with the computers. The sounds indicated machine behavior, clicks and taps and keyboard strokes. A little bell when something downloaded or perhaps deleted.

"I sensed him getting closer. Why him? Why not her? Most hired assassins are male. Who told me that? I was thinking a little randomly at this point. I started trying to figure things out. Had the hacker hired this murder? Were they just two players in a much larger plot, or was it really just Jimmy hiring a hit man after all? Or Abby? My mind flooded with thoughts, my ears roared. I was afraid. I smelled him taking a step down the hall toward me. He wasn't hiding his footfalls. He didn't know I was there. He was moving more quickly now. Job done. Almost.

"I remember thinking *What else does he have to do? What does he need in the bedroom? Get out of here, buddy, or you'll be busted*. Or dead. My trigger finger found its home. I raised my gun arm aiming at the air just inside the bedroom door. The tap from the bathroom sink gushed, and I almost pulled the trigger. I managed to stop myself in time, while alarm breezed through my body. I gave myself commands. Breathe. Think. Plan. I assumed he was wearing gloves. So why the water? What was he washing if not his hands?

"After the water stopped, he walked away from me, and I almost sagged to the floor in relief. No police at the scene yet, but maybe they'd catch him outside the building. After a little while, I went and sat on the bed and waited until you got there. It seemed like you arrived after hours, but it was more like thirty minutes, start to finish."

Paxton said thanks and took me back to my vehicle. By the time I returned from making my formal statement, it was late afternoon. I immediately swallowed a dose of my meds, hoping for anxiety relief. Too much anxiety blows up into panic, and panic sets the stage for a PTSD episode. I had not signed up for this stress, this awful witnessing of murder, of death. I'd trained in finding missing persons, who were almost all alive and healthy when I found them. The few deaths I'd had to report had been from natural causes, and the dead bodies had been remote, reported to me from a police blotter in another state. Along with finding missing persons, I did insurance fraud work. I followed people and taped them. I was good at these things.

I was not good at murder. None of my clients before Jimmy Heyl had been suspected of murder. Murder was supposed to have stayed buried with my past. But it had followed me. Was it any wonder I was resorting to medication again? And did using benzodiazepine mean I was no longer in recovery? What about the episode I'd had last night? These were questions for a trained professional, and as the pill kicked in and my head stopped replaying the moment Kennedy fell, I decided a little blue football-shaped pill would be okay here or there until my next appointment with Dr. Cam on Monday.

I was home now. Safe. I'd get through the night just fine. Tomorrow was another story, but since the police didn't seem worried about Kennedy and Roseann's co-workers, maybe I could use my skills tracking missing persons to find them. I especially wanted to find the pregnant one.

I'd switched my phone to silent at the police station. When I reached for it to turn it on, I noted several missed calls from Jimmy. Before I could return the calls, my phone rang. Jimmy. My client. A murder suspect. I answered the phone.

Jimmy sounded wildly subdued. I pictured him behind his closed office door in the house, his kids and grandkids all there. Everyone in tears or eating casseroles from the neighbors. So he was agitated, but he didn't want the family to know. "There are photos of some machine, a cherry picker. There's film of the Flatiron, with a close-up of the bullet hole in somebody's window!" Jimmy said. "A single white male, they're saying. If that's Kennedy—and how many single white guys live at the Flatiron? It's all married people with kids. And 99 percent of them are black. So it's Kennedy. I know it is. The cops are going to pin that one on me too! You gotta find the guy who did this."

"You have an alibi for Roseann's murder." I didn't mention the hit man angle.

"Yeah, well, about that." Jimmy sounded less belligerent, more tentative.

"What?" A bad feeling stirred in the pit of my stomach.

"Okay, I might have slipped out of the bar for a bit last night."

"When?"

"During the time Roseann was killed."

I bit back a bad word. "Why didn't you tell me? Where did you go?"

"To the opera."

I wasn't sure I was hearing right, but I grabbed a pen and paper and started taking notes. "Opera. Got it. Anybody see you there?"

"I—this does not sound good, but I kept a low profile. I wore a hat. I saw a few people, made sure they didn't see me."

"What kind of hat?"

He hesitated. "A black beret," he finally admitted.

I had the urge to laugh, which is unusual for me in most situations, but the pill must have been hitting me pretty hard. That or the visual of Jimmy in a beret. At the opera. If it was even true.

"Was your car in the parking lot?" I was pretty sure the Opera House had video surveillance. It would be easy to prove Jimmy, beret and all, had been there when Roseann was being killed. I shivered and eyed my bottle of miracle medication hoping it would last me until Monday. I would need a refill.

"I Ubered. The Caddy was in Corktown all night. Which is why my alibi was solid. That bitch."

"Wait? Who?"

"Abby. Never mind."

My suspicious mind whirred. Jimmy hadn't ever adequately explained why he'd had no interest in the stalker. What if that was because he'd hired the guy to follow and then kill his wife and her lover? And now he was being evasive, didn't want to explain why Abby had changed her alibi. He'd lied to me about his whereabouts at the time of the murder, at the very least.

"Why lie about it? And why tell me now?" I wanted to believe what my gut was telling me, that despite everything, his two-timing, his spying, his lies, he was innocent. "You're from Grosse Pointe. Don't you people do stuff like go to the opera all the time?"

"I could only get one ticket, and Roseann would have been pissed." Jimmy's voice broke a little when he said his wife's name. "She loved Puccini."

Just then, he didn't sound like a guy who'd killed his wife. "So what happened? Why give a false alibi in the first place?" If he kept evading, I'd quit the case. Hell, maybe I should be rethinking my entire line of work. More to share with Dr. Cam on Monday.

"It's crazy. I know. I had the whole thing set up. Abby thought I had to take Roseann to the opera; Roseann thought we couldn't get tickets. Then Abby said she's going back in to the PD to change her story. She's on a rampage because I can't see her for a while. Kids in town. Mourning to do." He took in an audible breath, then resumed. "You have no idea how stressful it is having two wives—well, Abby only thinks she's my wife—not that I pretended to marry her or anything. She's the one who's pretending. Not anymore, though."

I didn't say anything. I was thinking about how I was going to get Jimmy out of this and if I even wanted to anymore, the lying, cheating jerk.

"Listen, White, I loved them both, God's honest truth. The cops are going to get this all wrong. I'm an easy one to pin this on."

My warring brain punched aside my reservations

once again. It was true Jimmy had the right to hire a good PI if he didn't think the police would dig deep enough to prove his innocence. And he was still my client. If he was telling the truth about being at the opera. "What brand of vodka do you drink again? Did you have any that night? At the opera?"

"Yeah, I had a couple of pops." He rattled off the name of his pricey booze, and I jotted it down. "You believe me, right? You're going to keep looking for the guy? Whoever he is?"

I sidestepped the part about believing him. "Sure, I'll stay on the case." He might be a liar and a two-timing cheater, but I just didn't see Jimmy hiring a hit man. The thought of it didn't ring true. Why would he insist I find the killer on his dime if the guy could simply turn around and finger Jimmy?

"I'm going to look into this on one condition."

"Name it."

"You tell me right now—no bullshit—why you blew it off when I told you Roseann had a stalker."

"Okay, all right, simmer down. It's simple, really. Just kind of embarrassing. I thought it was my brother."

Jimmy went on to tell me about how his little brother Danny had always had a crush on Roseann. "Since high school, I shit you not." And how Jimmy had told Danny he thought Roseann was fooling around with somebody at work. Danny swore Roseann would never do anything like that. "He thinks she's a goddess. Was. Damn it, I can't believe she's gone, White." Finally, Jimmy surmised, when I mentioned a stalker, that Danny had been up to his old tricks. "He used to follow her home from choir practice, peek in her bedroom window at night when he was a kid. When I found out about it, I kicked his ass, and he stopped all that shit." Jimmy had assumed that now Roseann was cheating on him, Danny was back to his old tricks.

"Okay," I said. "Did you tell the police this?"

"Hell no. I'm not ratting out my own brother. Who's innocent, by the way. I asked Danny about it a few days ago, when Roseann was still alive, and he swore to me he hadn't been stalking her. He's taking her death hard."

"Fine." I could see how Jimmy had kept his suspicions about Danny to himself out of some misguided sense of sibling loyalty. "I'll look into the opera but it's not going to matter where you were if the stalker was a hit man."

"It will prove to you I'm not lying. And you can tell your boyfriend Paxton."

I let the Paxton comment slide. "Take a photo of yourself right now with that beret on and email it to me. After that, I'll get proof you were at the opera."

"Okay, fine." One point for Jimmy. He hadn't claimed the beret was no longer in his possession. "Can you find out if the other dead one is Kennedy?"

"Why? So you can worry more? Just try to stay calm for your kids and your grandkids. You'll find out when the rest of the world does."

"You're coming to the funeral, right?"

"I'll be there." Roseann would be buried on Wednesday. "But I should have a witness proving you were at the opera before then."

I live in a hotel attached to a casino, but I don't go to that part of the building much. Not a gambler, at least with money. Still, I've made friends with most of the staff, so it was no big deal for me to go into one of the bars on the premises and ask the bartender if he got many orders for Jimmy's expensive vodka.

He pulled a clear, skull-shaped bottle off the shelf. Same bottle Jimmy had used last night at Abby's place. The casino's bottle was almost full. "Not much call for this one. It's pricey. Want a shot? On the house." I'd helped Jesse figure out who'd been skimming tips when I'd first moved in, and he had a soft spot for me.

"Wish I could," I said. "Working." Sure, I'd had a pill, but that only made it possible for me to dial down to normal. Alcohol would increase the effects.

"Maybe later," he said.

I waved goodbye without promising anything.

It was maybe three o'clock in the afternoon. I doubted the bartender at the opera house would be on duty. But I drove there anyway because I needed a name. That took twenty minutes including driving time. I'm youngish, and sometimes, like today, that can be an advantage. Once I assured him (with a bright smile) I wasn't poaching one of his employees, but in fact wanted to deliver a valuable item to the bartender who'd worked last night, the manager currently working the opera house floor slipped me a name and address. I didn't mention the item in question was valuable only to Jimmy and was in fact not a material object but a positive identification.

The bartender lived in a row of nice condos in the New Center area. Across the street, some factory or other had been blasted, and the rubble remained. Nice view if you like dystopia. Maybe why a bartender could afford such a beauty of a condo. I rang the bell, and Eduardo Enez answered after a brief delay in which he was probably checking me out from his peephole. I was in jeans and a T-shirt and had carefully reapplied my makeup before I left the casino so it looked like I didn't have any on. Fresh scrubbed and innocent, that's me. The *I'm not here to deport you, I'm from Publisher's Clearinghouse* look had served me well in the past.

"Hi. Eduardo Enez? I'm here because my dad forgot to tip you last night, and he felt terrible about it. He wanted me to give you something." That got Eduardo onto the porch. "This"—I held a fifty-dollar bill aloft, just out of Eduardo's reach—"is for you if you can tell me what this guy was drinking last night." I showed the snap Jimmy had emailed me.

"Shining Skull," Eduardo said. "He had three. Only person drinking it all night."

"Well, from what I understand, he forgot to tip you for the last drink."

Eduardo pretended to contemplate that, but I was in a hurry to get home, so I tucked the bill into his shirt pocket. He smiled his bartender smile, and I waved goodbye.

I stopped for a cold-brew coffee on the way home because my meds, after they level me out, make me tired. After I ordered, I thought I would have been better off getting some food, but I was too tired. I drank the coffee as fast as I could without getting brain freeze, and by the time I got back to my suite, I'd perked up a bit. I was still hungry though. Luckily the casino had three restaurants, and they all delivered. Before I could call down an order, my doorbell chimed. I don't have any friends. Had to be Paxton. I let him in.

He looked good.

"Please tell me you are here to say you have found the pregnant co-worker and she's taking a leave of absence out of town."

"No."

"Well, I found out about Abby recanting her alibi for Jimmy. From Jimmy." The caffeine had done its work, and I quickly spun the story of my afternoon adventures. I even played the recording of Eduardo identifying Jimmy at the opera.

Paxton looked at me, clearly not impressed. Then he smiled. I avoided staring at his perfect teeth by closely analyzing his coffee cup. It was made to look like one of the cardboard ones, but it was actually reusable. Paxton was an environmentalist.

"I've seen Jimmy handle a weapon at the club, and the guy's a mediocre shot."

Paxton shook his head.

Paxton knew, and I knew. The murders were professional.

"I really don't think Jimmy hired anybody to kill his wife. He wants me to find the guy. Why would he want me to do that when it could implicate him?"

"You had dinner yet?" He had not answered my question.

"No. You?"

He shook his head.

"You want me to order us something?"

"Or we could go out." Paxton surprised me.

"You like coney dogs?" I said.

"Sure." He said he knew the best place in the city.

"Well then, let's go," I said. We went out to the hall, and I pushed the button for the elevator.

"You seem to have recovered from the events of this morning." We had the elevator to ourselves.

"Well, I am reconsidering my line of work," I

admitted. "But I'm okay. Hungry, is all."

"No panic? Fugue?"

Damn when he said it, it sounded bad. "Not today," I said. Okay, so technically, I am a bit of a head case, but I'm getting better. Things with my client are getting worse, but I am better. I put my hand out and held it steady. "Not even the shakes."

"You're fine," he said, opening the passenger door of his car for me. "Good work tracking down the bartender," he said as he slid behind the wheel.

"Not that it matters." I said what I knew he was thinking.

Instead of starting the car, he was looking at me, some kind of intense look. "This is just between us," he said.

What was he talking about? What was between us? I got very still. Yes, there was something there, in the few feet of air that separated us, a low hum, insistent, without sound. It had been there from the day I met Paxton; I usually ignored it.

"Okay?" he said, turning over the motor and pulling out of the casino's portico.

I realized there was no "us." He meant he was going to share something confidential with me about the case. *I'm an idiot*.

"Absolutely," I said, my voice smooth as I could make it.

"Your client may be a really bad guy. You need to be very careful."

We drove to whatever secret location Paxton knew that housed the best coney dogs in the city.

I couldn't let the Jimmy thing drop. "I don't think it's Jimmy."

"You got a soft spot for con artists?"

"Well, my dad was one."

He nodded.

"So why do you guys think Jimmy did it? What's the proof?"

"I can't tell you that. But we have compelling evidence that leads me to believe this guy could be a danger to you."

"Why can't you tell me what you have on him?"

He sighed. "It's confidential."

I didn't say anything. We drove in silence for a few minutes. Finally, Paxton said "At this point, the only thing that's going to help Jimmy is a squeaky-clean search of his financials."

"So my theory about the murders being work-related? Something to do with that hacking problem Kennedy and Roseann were working on?"

"It's a decent theory, but the department likes a less-complicated one." He turned down a side street. We were in a part of town I was not familiar with, but I recognized the new bridge over Mexicantown.

If my decent theory turned out to be incorrect, I'd get serious about a change in career. I knew I didn't want to deal with homicide, but it's not like you can have the client sign an agreement that there will be no murder or mayhem on the case. This was probably a rare instance. I'd be back to routine insurance fraud with the occasional missing persons mixed in soon. The job was all I had, and I had put some serious years, a major chunk of my twenties, into it.

Paxton pulled up to the curb. We walked a few buildings down to a noisy, crowded diner. We took the last free seats at the counter and through the large plate-glass window, watched the sun go down on the glittering gritty city.

Chapter 8

Paxton

When Paxton had a homicide to solve, he thought of nothing else. He worked twenty-hour days, didn't eat much. So why was he sitting in a diner in a sketchy part of town with Lily White, watching the sunset? She'd asked for coney dogs, so he'd taken her to Ned's Coney Island. The thought of a chili dog woke his taste buds. He needed to eat. That's why he was here with her. No other reason.

Instead of trying to come up with conversation, like he would have to do if this were an actual date, he was silent, his gaze wandering to a couple crossing the street toward the diner. Behind them were boarded-up and tagged buildings that had once been part of a vibrant shopping area. And not that long ago.

"When I was a kid, my mom took me school shopping over there," he told Lily. "I got my black loafers, my navy-blue slacks, my white shirt, my ties. We ordered jackets from the school."

"Sounds like a private school."

He nodded. He hadn't thought about what it sounded like. If he had, he wouldn't have spoken.

"Was Kennedy and Roseann's co-worker pregnant?"

"We'll follow it up, but our investigation is leaning

another way."

"You mean you still think Jimmy did it."

"It's too soon to say." But he said that just to be kind. Bingo was a hit man, probably working for Diablo, the baddest ass in Detroit. Jimmy knew that and had hired Bingo to kill his wife. Some things were simple. Others, like why he was being so soft on Lily White, had more tangles.

"So why didn't you follow up on the sheet of paper in the dead man's hand?"

"I will. I had a witness to interview, an autopsy to attend, a cherry picker to track down, files to read, a team meeting to lead, a report to write, a chief to brief."

"Your dad?" Lily asked. Paxton scanned carefully for any judgment in her voice. Didn't find it.

He hadn't meant to say all that. "Yeah," he said, then closed his mouth.

"So you found the cherry picker?"

He nodded.

"Where was it?"

"On a side street behind the library. Nice houses, Wayne State neighborhood. It was parked next to a tree." It wasn't classified information. She'd read it in the paper if he didn't tell her. The other thing, about Bingo and Jimmy's connection, that would not be in the paper. It didn't prove anything. At this point, it was a compelling coincidence.

"So you still think Jimmy hired the hit?" She had lowered her voice considerably.

"Some new facts have come to light."

The counter guy set their orders down. She took a bite of her coney instead of probing him with questions about the new facts. The place, despite its dicey location, was packed with a line out the door. People actually came from the suburbs to eat here. And after a game? Forget it. The line went practically to Mexicantown. He inhaled his first coney dog and took a bite of the second.

As he chewed, his eyes found the couple he'd seen crossing the street. They were in a small knot of people forming at the door. Two guys moved up the sidewalk to join the short line outside. One of them was limping. Bingo.

Like the dullard he was, Bingo made no effort to hide out. Probably thought Diablo would protect him. Paxton grabbed his wallet, threw some money down on the counter, and turned toward Lily. Her focus moved from the money on the counter to his unfinished meal to his eyes.

"I have to leave," he said. "Stay here and out of the way of that window."

Her eyes widened. She nodded, but when he got up and started toward the door, she was right behind him. He decided not to make any moves that would alarm Bingo, so he didn't turn around. He had Bingo in his sights; the hit man wasn't looking inside the diner but scanning out across the street. Six or seven people crowded the open door.

"The one with the limp, am I right?" Lily's voice was barely a whisper as they slid through the folks at the door.

She'd spotted Bingo. Remembered the limp from her own surveillance. He nodded once. No unnecessary movement. Nothing to attract attention as Bingo's eyes swept the line they were now moving discreetly through, scanned past them without interest to a patrol car on the street. Bingo didn't run when he saw the police unit, but he looked ready.

"Yes." Paxton answered Lily's question and moved next to her, his arm around her, his face turned into her ear, whispering to her like a lover. Like any guy on a date on Saturday night. "Stay out of this," he murmured, before he gently thrust her behind him, strode out four long steps, nobody between him and Bingo. He pulled out his department issue Smith and Wesson and aimed at Bingo still walking. "Stay where you are. Police. Hands up."

In those four strides to Bingo, he'd noted he had a clear shot. Nobody coming up behind Bingo to join the line in front of the diner. Nobody to get in Bingo's way as he made a run for it. If there was panic in the diner behind Paxton, he didn't hear it. Time was moving in slow-mo now, like it always did when he confronted a suspect. As Bingo and his buddy took off, heading north, Paxton was right behind them. Sirens blared, then several things happened at once. Paxton caught Bingo by the waistband of his jeans just as he saw Lily fly by, chasing Bingo's pal, brandishing a pink .38 and yelling about a citizen's arrest. Paxton cuffed Bingo as the squad car pulled onto the street with a screech of wheels.

"Suspect in the double homicide at the Flatiron," Paxton said, handing Bingo off to the first uniform out of the car while he took off after Lily and Bingo's friend.

"We recognized him from the APB," the second uniform yelled at Paxton.

"Take him downtown," Paxton called over his shoulder, running fast to catch up to Lily. He hadn't heard any shots fired from her ridiculous weapon, and as he passed her, he yelled for her to put the gun away and let the police handle things. Then he turned the corner and got Bingo's friend by the collar. He hauled him over to the second squad car that had arrived on the scene and parked parallel to the first car. He holstered his weapon.

A uniform cuffed the Mexican guy. "He was heading toward Clark Park," Paxton said. Once both men were secured in the backs of separate squad cars, Paxton gave the uniforms a rundown. "Suspected shooter showed up to have dinner with a friend. Maybe Bingo has been staying with him in Mexicantown. Maybe we'll get lucky and find the weapon from the homicides when we get this guy's name and address."

One uniform was writing everything down while the rest of them listened.

"Take them downtown," Paxton said, "I'm right behind you."

As the patrol cars screeched away, the scene sped up for Paxton. People were screaming and crying and carrying on. One woman had fainted. Lily was nowhere. Damn. Had she suffered another panic attack? He couldn't leave until he found her, made sure she was okay. She'd been ready to risk her life. As much as he needed to go, he needed to stay for one minute more.

"Everything's fine, folks. We have arrested someone, and he is in police custody."

He phoned Nigel and told him to meet him downtown at the first precinct. "Wear plain clothes," Paxton said.

The crowd shouted questions at him as he moved through them, looking for Lily. She wasn't anywhere.

He made calming gestures with his hands but kept on the move, down the street to where he'd parked. She was sitting on his back bumper like it was a tailgate party. Relief flooded him.

"You okay?"

"Fine. You?" Paxton shoved his fingers across his close-cropped hair, rubbing at his meticulously razored side part.

Lily eyed him with curiosity. "You couldn't mess up your hair if you tried," she said. Then, "I'm good. Guess I better find another ride home, huh?" Lily stood.

"I'll drop you."

"But that was your shooter. You need to question him."

"He'll wait."

Paxton noticed Lily looked a bit wobbly now that she'd gotten to her feet. He opened his arms and grabbed her to his chest. She collapsed into him. He felt her arms come around him. She pressed her face into his shoulder.

"I'm so glad you're okay," she said. She squeezed him tighter and looked up into his eyes.

At that moment, when their eyes met, he realized she had not needed propping up. Lily was fine. This was something else. He didn't have time to figure it out. He kept one arm around her tightly, opened the passenger door with the other, and released his grip on her shoulder. She eased into the seat without complaint.

"It's registered," she said, when he'd buckled himself in and put the car in drive. "The .38."

"Yes, I know." Paxton had a list of Lily's registered weapons. There'd been a .38 in the mix, but he hadn't known it would be pink.

"Yep. Pink. A mistake. But it fits inside this purse better than the Beretta." She held up her tiny shoulder bag. "And you still have my other guns."

"Thanks for your help," he said. If she hadn't stayed on the Mexican's tail, he might have lost his best chance at recovering the murder weapon.

"No problem," she said.

They spent the last few minutes of the ride in silence. They'd had fun. He could tell she thought so, too. She wasn't fearful; she was jazzed. He pulled up at the hotel entrance, waving away the valet. He wanted to walk her to her door, to see her safely inside. He couldn't. He had work to do. Even this ten-minute detour had been unwise. Hell, most of what he did when he was with her was unwise.

"I'll see you around, Paxton," Lily said as the valet opened her door. She turned to him and smiled before she took the valet's extended arm and exited his vehicle.

By the time Paxton got to the First Precinct, the Mexican had been identified and had consented to a search of his premises. Paxton sent the second squad of uniforms off with a description of Bingo's takedown rifle and silencer. Bingo had been processed and was cooling his heels in an interrogation room. Nigel was there, in a suit and tie. Paxton hadn't changed either; he was still in his work clothes. When he was on a case, he lived in work clothes.

"Hey," Paxton said, shaking Nigel's hand. "Thanks for getting down here so quickly."

"I live in the area," Nigel said.

Paxton should have figured. Lots of the young white cops were moving back into the city. And not just cops. Quite a few millennials seemed to think Detroit was the place to be, including Lily.

"You get the basics from the uniforms for the report?"

Nigel nodded.

"This afternoon," Paxton said, "I didn't have time to fill you in before your shift ended." The uniforms were listening. That was fine. They were part of this now, too. He clicked on the notes he kept on his phone.

"Bingo's limp. He got that from a bullet fired in a bar brawl. The altercation was in Grosse Point. At a bar Jimmy Heyl—he's the husband of the Friday night vic," Paxton added for the uniforms, "owned with his brother."

"And we've got a connection," Nigel said.

"Yes, we do, and while it's promising, it's still circumstantial." Paxton took a breath. "What would be ideal, but probably too much to hope for, is Bingo IDing Heyl tonight as the guy who hired him to kill his wife and her lover."

Then Paxton spelled it out for Nigel, who would interrogate with him, and the uniforms, who would surely watch through the two-way window. "We have Bingo on film shooting the weapon that has resulted in two homicides. This is currently our one solid piece of evidence. I would like the weapon, or a signed confession, plus a positive ID of Jimmy Heyl, but we can't count on any of that. Still, going in, the film is very good. And crime scene's going over that cherry picker at the lab right now with every one of their fancy tools."

"He have a clue he's going down for double homicide tonight?" Nigel asked.

Paxton shook his head. "Despite being ex-military, which is where he learned to shoot, he's not very smart, so it's possible he doesn't understand that yet, despite being charged. Bingo's done time for that altercation at Heyl's bar in Grosse Point. He shot first. And the guy ended up losing a leg. Which is why Bingo went to prison. But he got off light—an illegal weapons charge, intent to do bodily harm. So he may feel like this is just going to be another thing like that. We have to let him know that, this time, he'll be going down for a very long time. And his incarceration won't be in the country-club joint where they stowed him last time."

"We get him to see it's in his best interests to ID the person who hired him."

"That is our goal, yes," Paxton said.

"Understood," Nigel said.

To Paxton, Nigel seemed determined, his adrenaline under control. He'd do. They went in, and Nigel hit record on the videotape machine in the corner. When Paxton and Nigel sat down across from Bingo, the shooter looked defiant.

"You can't prove nothing," he said.

Paxton turned to Nigel. "He get his phone call?" Paxton knew he had. Nigel had fully briefed him. But he liked that Bingo seemed in a mood to talk. Maybe this reminder would do the trick. If Nigel picked up on the unspoken idea that they'd give the guy enough rope to hang himself.

"Yep," Nigel said.

"It was a setup!" Bingo said. "That number was good yesterday."

"Prepaid phone," Nigel explained. "Voice mail. Recorded message of the Joker off one of the Batman movies, laughing that crazy laugh." Nigel kept his eyes on Bingo, but he'd played along perfectly with Paxton, reminding Bingo that his partner in crime was suddenly gone and ready to let Bingo take the rap alone.

"So you got burned?" Paxton took a stab.

He and Nigel had briefly discussed the idea that Heyl, or whoever had hired Bingo, was setting him up to take the fall solo. This made Paxton further wonder if perhaps the cherry picker had been left in plain sight because there'd be some kind of DNA or other evidence to connect the hits to Bingo.

"I need another phone call. My lawyer," Bingo said.

"Nope." That was Nigel, playing bad cop.

"I'm not saying nothing then."

"Maybe we can help you out, Bingo. After you help us." Paxton tapped the folder Nigel had laid on the table between them.

Bingo shrugged.

"He doesn't get it—that he was set up," Nigel said.

"We know somebody hired you, and probably promised you a lot of money, to do this job, Bingo." And Paxton was betting Bingo hadn't gotten paid. Just another reason to give Bingo up to the cops once the job was done.

"You know how hard it is for an Indian ex-con to get a job?" Bingo whined.

Paxton nodded, keeping his face neutral but feeling disgust twist his gut.

"You picked the wrong profession, Bingo," Nigel said.

"I'm a better marksman than you," Bingo said to Nigel.

"We have evidence that proves you murdered two people in the last twenty-four hours. That's double homicide."

"What evidence?" Bingo was a shade less belligerent.

"We've got it on tape, Bingo. The crime being committed. The stalking before that." Also bullet casings from both homicides likely from the same weapon, but they'd save that.

"I want a lawyer. I'm not saying anything until I get a lawyer. There ought to be a law about videotaping somebody without his permission."

Nigel and Paxton both looked at Bingo for a long minute.

Finally, Nigel spoke. "I put in a call to your parole officer. He's going to get you sorted. Your attorney will see the video footage of you stalking and then killing Roseann Heyl. You're going to be denied bail on the strength of that tape," Nigel said. "And by the way, you won't be doing your time at Peckingham again."

"You can't harass me like this. I don't have to say another word until my lawyer gets here."

"You're right. You don't have to say anything. But let me go over everything we have once more, so you don't miss anything that's happening here," Paxton said. He kept his voice low and his eyes on Bingo as he shook his head slowly, like he was sorry to be the one to share the bad news. "A witness videotaped the first murder. You used the same weapon for both hits. We found the cherry picker, and we're within minutes of finding your rifle. Mexicantown, right?"

Bingo flinched.

"That's a big slice of solid evidence," Paxton said.

Technically, only one piece of evidence would hold up in court at this point, but they were working on the other pieces that would nail Bingo's coffin shut. By Bingo's reaction to "Mexicantown," Paxton was hopeful they'd have the murder weapon tonight.

"We're not sure why you followed Roseann around for a week before you shot her, but maybe you aren't either. It sounds like whoever hired you wasn't exactly a trustworthy partner." Nigel again, sneering.

"Thing is," Paxton said, "none of this was your idea. You were hired to do a job; you did it. We want the person who hired you. He's going down for double homicide." This time, Paxton left out the part about Bingo being implicated as well.

"You got the message during your phone call. The guy who hired you to commit these crimes is laughing at you. Why should you protect him?" Nigel said.

Paxton tapped the file. They let the silence hang.

Finally, Bingo cracked. "I don't know who he is!"

It wasn't a confession to pulling the trigger, but it was close.

"Can you identify him from a photo?" Paxton opened the file and showed him an enlarged driver's license photo of Jimmy Heyl.

Bingo shook his head. "I never saw him. Only talked to him on the phone."

"You're lying," Nigel said. Then he got up and left the interrogation room, slamming the door.

Bingo's eyes widened. "Where's he going?"

Paxton shrugged. He knew Nigel was headed into the next room where he could watch Paxton coax something, anything, out of Bingo. If Paxton was very lucky, and Nigel was on his wavelength, his new partner was also getting some kind of voice recording on tape. Anybody's voice.

"So how did you get paid?" Paxton asked, playing his hunch.

"I never got paid! He—this is what he did. He paid me to follow the woman. A hundred bucks a night. No harm, right?"

"How'd you get paid?"

"Wired into my bank account. Almost a grand, just for walking around."

"For stalking."

"Well, I didn't think of it that way."

"I need your banking information."

"I don't—I, ah, I go to a check-cash place. Not an actual bank, per se."

"Let me guess. Diablo's store."

"Yeah, so?"

Paxton was silent a beat. He had a friend working inside Diablo's organization. Deep undercover. FBI. But he wouldn't contact the guy unless it was essential. The FBI had been building their case for years, and he wouldn't endanger his friend by asking for special favors.

"Then he said I could make ten times that if I killed her. And ten times that if I killed her boyfriend, too."

"Did he say that? *Her boyfriend*?"

"Yep."

"But no more money came into your account?"

"No."

"Not even after you shot both of them?"

"I'm not answering that," Bingo said.

Nigel came back into the room. Bingo looked like a puppy about to get kicked.

"This might be your lucky night, Bingo," Nigel said. He held his phone up in the air and smiling, bad-cop demeanor gone.

"Is it him?"

"It might be," Nigel said.

He pressed play, and a disembodied voice came into the room. "Yeah, right, be there," the voice said, then a dial tone.

"Is that your boss, Bingo? What's his name anyway?"

"I didn't know his name. He wanted us to call him Kid OK. Can you play that again?"

Paxton caught the "us" but sat back and let Nigel have a go. He had not been wrong about Nigel. He was grateful to his father for fast-tracking a provisional promotion. Just this case, then they'd see how it played, the chief had said to Paxton's request for a partner.

Nigel played the recording again.

"Yeah, that might be him."

Bingo's parole officer showed up before he finished talking, looked none too pleased. He requested a private chat, and Paxton and Nigel got up to leave. On their way out the door, Nigel locked down the video recorder, and Paxton swept up the file that had only contained one thing. Heyl's photo ID blown up to 8 × 10 inches.

"So who was the voice on the phone?" Paxton asked Nigel after the door had clicked shut.

"Cranbil."

Paxton snorted. Cranbil was one of the uniforms who'd taken in Bingo. Which meant Bingo didn't know anything or wasn't being truthful but probably both.

"The guy is about as trustworthy as a three-dollar

bill."

"Did you hear him say 'us' when he talked about Kid OK? Like there are more just like Bingo sitting around waiting to kill people for money that never shows up?"

"Yeah, and he referred to Roseann Heyl as Kennedy's 'girlfriend' while I was out of the room. I caught that on the two-way."

"We need to request Bingo's 'bank' records from Diablo's store. If we can match up the dates of the transfers from Heyl's bank to Bingo's, we may have a shot at solving this thing. And we should get a tape of Heyl's voice," Paxton said.

Nigel looked pained, but he nodded.

"Tomorrow's fine for the bank records," Paxton said. "And we can get a recording of Heyl's voice at the funeral next week. You go on home for tonight. I'm going to wait to see if the rifle comes in."

He noted by his watch that it was closer to tomorrow than he'd imagined. Nigel left, and Paxton took the report from Cranbil. He scanned it, but either the uniforms had not noticed Lily's part in tonight's capture or they had smoothed it out of the official record. Fine by him. He didn't need his father, or anybody else, giving him grief about hanging out with a PI.

Chapter 9

Lily

I got through the next few days, through the constant replaying of Roseann, dead, as I bent over her and Kennedy shot before my eyes, the blood oozing out of their heads, their eyes open, but nothing there. In the mix was my cousin, the man who had raped me, the man I shot dead myself defending another young woman from his predatory ways. I had left that chapter of my life behind, or so I thought. I could cope with the memories of Kennedy and Roseann, but when my cousin's face, my cousin's blood, entered the gory mix, the only way I could deal was with double doses of heavy meds. Monday, Dr. Cam had given me new prescriptions.

I needed a double session with Dr. Cam after Sunday, the worst day of my new life. On Sunday, I hadn't left my suite. Had my food delivered. Didn't eat much of it. The phone never rang. Paxton never knocked. It was just me and the bloody thoughts in my head. Work was always my savior, but I didn't want to venture out of my suite and I didn't know what else to do for Jimmy from inside the hotel.

Paxton had hinted at something. He'd said "new facts had come to light." I'd pressed Jimmy about Bingo. I'd shown Jimmy Bingo's picture. Said Bingo had a limp from a gunfight years ago. Did he know the guy? Did the story ring any bells? Jimmy said no, nothing he could think of, but I caught some hint, even over the telephone, that maybe Jimmy was leaving ingredients out again. Then I'd told myself, no, Jimmy was thinking about his family. Focused on his wife's funeral.

I spent Sunday night looking through old newspaper stories about Bingo. Finally, I found it. The bar Bingo got shot up at was owned by Jimmy and his brother. I hadn't even known Jimmy ever owned a bar, let alone the bar where Bingo had committed the crime that landed him in jail. Why hadn't Jimmy told me this? Did he think nobody would remember? Certainly, this was at least part of Paxton's "new information."

Paxton was probably thinking Jimmy knew Bingo, knew he was a marksman, knew he was out on parole and needed money. Could it be possible Jimmy'd hired Bingo? You bet. He could have hired him to follow Roseann around, just like he hired me. But then he gave Bingo an additional assignment. Why would he do that knowing I was filming the whole thing? It didn't quite add up, and I was not going to say anything else to Jimmy until his wife's funeral was over.

Monday, I focused on my own mental health. I went to yoga class and then kept my appointment with Dr. Cam. She specialized in rehabbing people with PTSD who were not military, who were not law enforcement, just ordinary people who were victims of violence. Like me. She suggested I find a new career after I told her what had happened over the weekend. I said I'd think about it, but it had taken a long time and a lot of work to get my PI license. I had developed certain skills, especially locating missing persons. Especially catching people pretending to be injured partying like it was 1999 on film. More than anything, I wanted to be normal. I didn't want to be fragile. I wanted to be tough. Could she help me toughen up? She said she thought I should go back on the other meds that had pulled me through last time. She had a cocktail for me of antidepressants, sleeping pills, and anti-anxiety meds. I said I didn't need the antidepressant, even though she reminded me it worked for anxiety, too. But I had not been born anxious. Life had made me anxious. People dying made me anxious. And sleepless. I didn't like taking so many pills; they made me feel like a loser. It was a dilemma.

Tuesday, I bought a new gun. Another Sig because who knew when I'd get mine back. Filled out paperwork. I didn't need another weapon, but being armed made me feel safe. Less anxious. Still no word from Paxton, but I figured that was good news. My client had not been arrested. They could not arrest him just because he owned a bar Bingo got shot in. Could they? They could get a search warrant, though. God knows what they'd find. I'd just have to sit tight to see what that would unearth, if anything.

When I saw Jimmy earlier today at Roseann's funeral, I didn't mention a thing about Bingo being at his bar when he got shot all those years back. I made it through the first hurdle of Wednesday: Roseann Heyl's Grosse Pointe Woods funeral mass. I'd learned nothing of note except Jimmy was beloved by his family and friends, and Abby had enough class to stay away. After formalizing my condolences in the receiving line, I headed down Jefferson along the Detroit River and into the city.

Kennedy was being buried at St. Ambrose.

I parked and searched among the dark-clothed flock for a pregnant woman whose face looked like the photo I'd snapped at the coffee shop in the Victory Motors building. I spotted only one who looked similar, and she was clearly pregnant this time. I assumed she must be the pregnant team member Kennedy had mentioned to me just before he died.

"I'm so sorry for your loss," I said, before the service began. "Lily White." I extended my hand, hoping she'd tell me her name. I needed to get her name and the name of the fourth member of the IT team working on the virus at Victory Motors. The names that Kennedy had never been able to give me.

"Melanie George." She put her hand, heavy and limp, in mine. "How did you know Tom?"

I squeezed her fingers lightly and let go. "I didn't really. I was investigating corporate espionage." The lie rolled off my tongue like truth, something I'm not proud of. "He was walking me through the easy stuff. I liked him though."

"Are you a cop?"

"No." I smiled. I used to be hard, or maybe brittle is a better word. Either way smiles didn't come naturally to me, even now. But something about a baby, even one not yet born, had a way of softening people, even bitter bitches like me. "Private investigator. I've been hired by Jimmy Heyl to find Roseann's and Tom's killer."

"Oh. I hope you do!"

"Have the police contacted you at all?"

"No. Why?"

"Just—you worked with Tom and Roseann." I guessed Paxton was right. My theory of a conspiracy involving computer hacking wasn't making a big impression down at the station. Just then I saw Paxton, standing in the back of the church. It was the first time I'd seen him since he dropped me off at the hotel Saturday night. My heart skidded into a kind of flutter, and I wondered if all the pills I'd been popping had done some kind of weird damage to my heart.

"Tom and Roseann were working on a worm or something—I'm sorry, is that the right word? Software hacking is not my game. Anyway, someone from your department, according to Tom, had slipped a virus into the system, and a group of you were working overtime to eradicate it before it infected the company worldwide."

Melanie nodded. "Yeah. Tom, Roseann, and me. Some management guys. Oh, and Eban Stern, but saying he was a hacker hunter was too generous."

"Why?"

"He was technically a part of the team, just like the management guys, but Eban was really just babysitting one of our vendors, A1 Automotive. They make components that interface with IT servers. Eban was dumbing it down for the engineers."

I keyed Eban Stern's name into my phone notes just as a priest in flowing robes wafted incense over Kennedy's coffin. Then he came down the aisle and did the same, gently swinging the censor on its chain at the rest of us.

Melanie must have gotten smoke in her eyes. She wiped tears from her cheeks with an old-fashioned cloth handkerchief. It was large, white, and square, monogrammed with a T and a K.

I put my arm around her and gave her a hug. I do not hug lightly, but this was a special situation. "Anybody know?" I'd made one of those leaps cops don't like. I don't know how I knew, I just did. Thomas Kennedy was Melanie George's baby daddy.

She shook her head, misery apparent in the sag of her neck and the tremble of her bottom lip. "How'd you guess?"

I nodded toward the hankie. "He spoke of you. He got a little shy when he said your name. He planned to visit the doctor with you. Those are his initials."

She swiped at her streaming eyes one last time before stowing the evidence. "We were planning a wedding. My family was coming from Alaska, and we had to wait for them to get the cash together or my mother would have been mad. Do you think my baby or me, are we targets?"

"Absolutely not. The killer is in jail." That much was true. But what about Victory Motors team? "Could you give me a list of the names of the management people on the hacker-hunter team?"

She took my phone, still open to the notepad, and keyed in three more names. I noted one was a woman and two were men. Now I knew who three of the people in that work photo were. Since management didn't tend to have coffee with IT geniuses, I figured the fourth to be Eban Stern. I'd look at all four of them. It was clear to me Melanie wouldn't have hired someone to shoot the father of her unborn child. I crossed her off my suspect list, and a chill ran up my arms when I remembered Kennedy had died shortly after I crossed him off my list. Maybe I'd hint to Melanie that she should go to Alaska for a nice long vacation.

"I haven't been reading the news or watching television. It seems like all I do is sleep. I miss him so much. Sometimes I dream about him, and he's still alive."

I patted her on the shoulder and gave her a little hug. Then, the service had started, and we both recited the words from our prayer books.

After mass, I walked out with Melanie. I glanced around, hoping to spot Paxton, but he'd vanished. Melanie and I stood as the pallbearers brought out the casket and slid it into a hearse. It was a lovely day. What a waste that Roseann and Kennedy had not lived to see it. Poor Melanie. I'd find out who was behind this for her sake if nothing else. My heart ached for Kennedy, who never got the chance to be a father to his unborn child.

I gave Melanie my card and told her to call me anytime, about anything. "Not just the case."

She hugged me, holding back what I sensed were large quantities of sobs. I wasn't one to make friends, but lately I'd been having all kinds of emotions, so maybe I needed to start. I felt like Kennedy was whispering in my ear, saying I owed him. I returned Melanie's hug as too few cars lined up behind the hearse.

"I just can't go to the grave," she said, finally letting me out of the hug.

"I know. It's okay." I mustered a smile.

"Good luck trying to get in to see management. Not one of them showed up here today. And neither did Eban." She sniffed.

"No respect," I said. "But they'll talk to me. Every

single one of them."

"Eban might not be that easy to find."

"Wait. Why? Won't he be at work?"

"No, that's right, I didn't get a chance to say. He quit yesterday."

"Before the problem with the software was solved?"

"That turned out to be a false trail. Roseann had found that out and sent a memo to me before she went to see—before she, before she…" Out came Kennedy's handkerchief and down poured the tears. I watched in dismay. I didn't understand the depth of her grief. I didn't understand the whole Victory Motors mess, but I knew one thing. I had to quit asking this poor woman questions that made her cry.

"Do you have a car?" Safe question.

"Yeah. I want to talk to some people from work, first, though."

"You sure you're okay?"

Melanie nodded.

"Please call me anytime if you need to," I said.

"You're the last person who saw him alive."

I nodded, accepting the strange status in her life. I eased out of the crowd and headed down Alter, where I'd parked, safely away from the hearse slowly starting the sad parade down East Jefferson.

When I got home, I Googled Eban Stern, but the guy who worked for the top automaker in the country didn't have so much as a LinkedIn profile. I didn't have any better luck tracking Stern down with any of the pricey search software I subscribed to, either. Why not? This was beginning to feel a bit like a skip trace, and that raised suspicions. I had been hired to find someone.

I was good at missing persons, having done extra training in this area after acquiring my PI license. I had never yet failed to find someone, even the ones who didn't want to be found, like the deadbeat dads who skipped town never to be heard from again. Or the biological parents of adults who had been adopted as children. I had found family members of all sorts. I had even found a few long-lost loves. I always worked the same way. Internet search, including social media, and subscription databases usually yielded at least an address. Talking to others who knew the missing person was also effective, but while I could go back to Melanie, she didn't sound like she'd been close to Stern.

I thought for a while. Then I called Victory Motors' human resources department. A woman with a vague air answered. I pictured her catching up on Facebook, as that was the level of attention her bored "HRhowcanIhelpyou?" conveyed.

"Hi," I said. "I hope you can help me."

Silence on the other end of the line. Single clicks of a computer every so often. Sounded like she was just browsing and not commenting. Okay.

"I have a check for one of your employees, Eban Stern in IT."

"How can I help you?"

"Well, Eban Stern quit Victory yesterday. I had his work address, and I thought I had his home address, but when I tried to deliver the check, it turned out I had the wrong home address. I must have written the number down wrong."

"We don't give out personal information—"

"Yes, I understand that. This is Shirley from A1

Automotive, and he's been helping us quite a bit. He did a little freelance work for us over a couple of weekends, and we wanted to compensate him."

A few clicks later, the HR rep rattled off his address and hung up. Just like that. The address was local and it was still early afternoon, so I grabbed my purse and got in my vehicle. I punched the address into the satnav and headed into the West Village. It was about the coziest neighborhood I'd seen in Detroit. Really good vibe. Lots of foot traffic. Restaurants, coffee shops, and small businesses with loft spaces on the second floors.

So many neighborhoods had that one bad house with a broken porch step and missing roof tiles. Vacant lots were not mowed. Try as they might, lots of folks had to deal with a city only half healed from the scars of a previous era.

But not so here. Fresh paint, clean brick, sparkling storefront windows. I found the loft Stern had been renting above an art supply store, parked, and walked up to the building. I wasn't sure what I expected from Stern. At this point, I was simply fishing for information from those closest to Roseann Heyl and Thomas Kennedy. Strange maybe to start with co-workers, but friends and family were all in deep mourning, and I was trying to be logical. Stern had not been at either funeral. Stern had been part of a small work team but almost as an adjunct to the core three. I could work management after I crossed Stern off my list.

Why was I so determined to find him? He had quit his job after two of his co-workers were murdered leaving no trace of himself on the Internet. He just seemed like a person of interest, as Paxton might say if he were not so intent on collaring my client. Once I eliminated Stern from any suspicion—after all, what possible motive would he have for killing his co-workers?—then I would question management and Heyl's brother.

Danny Heyl had had a lifelong crush on Roseann. Could that crush have morphed into some kind of insane jealousy? Seemed like a long shot. I'd checked out Danny Heyl at Roseann's funeral. He had been surrounded by family, all of whom had seemed equally as distraught as he did. Still, I liked to have a list. Maybe I'd put Danny before the management trio.

Except Eban didn't answer when I rang his upper flat from the bell at street level. There was no name next to the doorbell. No mailbox. I went into the art supply store. A woman in her mid-thirties wearing the kind of gauzy outfit one might expect in such a store came out from behind the sales counter. I was the only customer. She didn't seem overly eager to sell me easel and paint, just asked pleasantly if she could help.

"Yes, I hope so," I said. "I'm looking for Eban Stern, the tenant of the loft upstairs."

She looked mystified. "I own the building, and I live upstairs. With my partner."

"Eban?"

"No. I'm sorry. I've never heard of Eban Stern."

It wouldn't be the first time a skip had used more than one name, and it was now looking as if Eban Stern was officially a skip. I showed her the photo I'd taken the first day of my job following Roseann Heyl. Melanie had confirmed that Eban was the fourth person in the picture. I pointed him out to her. "Is this your partner?"

She looked at the photo, laughed, blushed, said no. "That is definitely not my wife," she said.

I nodded and tucked the photo into my purse. "Thanks for your help."

"No problem."

"Lovely store," I said. "I really like the neighborhood." I did, I thought, as I waved and exited. I got in my car thinking about how I liked the idea that she had her own business and she lived right above it and she could go to the restaurant on the corner for dinner whenever she didn't feel like cooking. If I was going to set up shop anywhere except in cyberspace where I currently advertised, I'd pick the West Village. I'd have an office on the main floor and live upstairs. Somehow, living adjacent to a casino didn't seem so perfect for me anymore. Weird. Yesterday, I'd loved it.

Back to the job at hand. Eban Stern had given a fake address. Victory Motors had failed to check that. Surely he'd have to have had a working phone number. I called Melanie as I climbed into my SUV. She answered right away.

"Hey, it's Lily. How're you holding up?"

"I know it's you. I programmed you into my phone. I'm okay." She sounded tired. Crying can wear a person out. Grief too.

"I'm sorry to bother you, but I wondered if you had Eban Stern's phone number?"

"Oh, yeah, sure." She sounded disappointed on top of tired now, but she didn't ask why I needed the number, just rattled it off while I keyed the sequence of numbers into my directory.

"Do you live anywhere near the West Village?" I

asked her. I felt like I shouldn't be all business. Not with her.

"I live *in* the West Village," she said. "Just off Kercheval."

"I love your neighborhood."

"It's a place to live."

"You want to grab lunch? I can't today, but maybe later this week?"

"That would be great." She still sounded tired but no longer disappointed. I'm not great at making friends, but I read people pretty well. Melanie needed a friend. According to my shrink, I did too. I'd been thinking Paxton could be the friend I was supposed to find, but it wouldn't hurt to have two friends.

"Get some rest. You sound like you could use it."

"I'm pretty tired."

"I hear it in your voice," I said. "I'll check in with you again tomorrow, okay?"

We hung up, and I wondered how I was going to fit friendship into my life. Paxton was easier in a way because we had the same dedication to similar jobs. It didn't feel so far afield. I tried to remember the last time I'd had a female friend. It had been a while, and even then, she'd been older, more like a big sister. But I was going to follow through. At this point, if Dr. Cam had told me I needed to take ballet lessons, I would have done it. Anything to regain a sense of control over my life, a sense that it was worth living, that I was a person worth something to somebody besides a client with a problem.

I got back to the hotel and as soon as I kicked off my shoes, I dialed the number Melanie had given me. Disconnected. Without an address, I had no way to talk to friends or family, no doors to knock on. This phone number was my last resort unless I wanted to call every Stern in the phone book. There were many. It would take days of the kind of rote task I liked least. Too bad I couldn't subpoena the phone records. But I had a friend who could. Paxton.

I sent him a text. *Saw you at the funerals today.*

I added a sad-face icon with a tear, which was not like me, but it's hard to figure out how to be with him.

He texted me right back. *What are you doing this afternoon?*

No plans.

Want to go for a boat ride?

I looked at my watch. It was that time of day between lunch and dinner that hung sort of heavy for me if I wasn't actively working. Sure, I could call every Stern in the book to ask if they were related to Eban. And I would. Tomorrow.

If I put off the dull chore until tomorrow and said yes to a boat ride, I would be following up on the mental-health-friend thing *and* working. I was just going to do it. Just ask Paxton to subpoena that phone record for me. I'd tell him why. He would have to admit this disappearing act by Eban Stern was weird.

Sure, I'd love to go out for a boat ride.

He asked me to meet him at the Yacht Club. I hung up feeling a lift of the heaviness that had weighed me down since Friday night. On top of the other things I would be accomplishing by meeting Paxton, I was also excited just to be out on the river. I adored the water. That had to be the reason I was feeling so happy after attending two funerals in one day.

Chapter 10

Paxton

Paxton had been ready to take out his dad's beautiful old boat when he got Lily's text. A ride on the river was the perfect antidote to funerals and to working nonstop for six days excluding a couple hours of sleep here and there when he could grab them. They'd done good work. Bingo had been useless as far as ID-ing whoever hired him, but he was the shooter in a double homicide and the press loved the fact that one less bad guy with a gun was roaming the city streets. Bingo was locked up in county jail until trial. He had not been granted bail.

Jimmy Heyl was another situation. His financials showed no hundred-dollar payment transfers. His phone records yielded no calls at all to Bingo. That wasn't saying the guy was in the clear, just that Paxton had to dig deeper. And he would. Tomorrow. Tonight, he was going to take a river ride with Lily. He wasn't concerned about it. Sure, the department would razz him no end for dating a PI. But he felt like Lily was just as low key as he was about any kind of relationship they might be forming. Nobody was going to see or hear anything from either of them about their business.

This would be the first time he'd had no ulterior motive for contacting her. It was a date, pure and simple. And Lily had agreed to it, so she must feel the same way he did. He liked her and wanted to get to know her better. Possibly much better.

Belle Isle was hopping today, with families barbecuing dinner, teenagers sunbathing, after-work boaters like him hitting the water. Lily hopped out of her SUV and walked up the dock to where Paxton stood. He smiled at her, and she smiled back.

"You smell so good," she blurted, stepping back when Paxton gave her a hug.

"Polo Red," he said, trying to decode Lily's mixed signals. He gave up and hopped aboard, handing her a rope out on the dock. He assumed she knew what to do with it, and she did, holding on and making sure the boat didn't bump the dock or drift out toward the river until they were ready.

Paxton did a quick check of the cruiser, satisfied that the chrome trim was shiny, the wood polished to a honeyed sheen. He'd spent an hour or so buffing it up, which he knew his dad would appreciate. The speed boat was Dad's pride and joy.

As Paxton took the rope from Lily, her hair whipped around her face. He tossed the rope into a cubby on the side of the boat and held out his hand for her to grasp as she climbed aboard. Once secure in the passenger seat, she flipped down the visor mirror, twisted her hair up, and tucked it into a clip.

"Need sunscreen?" Paxton asked, handing over a tube.

She took it and rubbed a bit onto her neck and nose. "I put stuff on my face at home," she explained.

He felt the last of the day's tension ease as he sat behind the wheel, taking his time heading through the no-wake zone, past the dock full of sailboats and speedboats and fancy fishing rigs.

Once on the river proper, he said, "Thought you might want to be on the water, seeing as that's where you're from. What's the name of your hometown again?"

"Doesn't matter." She laughed, but he knew she didn't like thinking about her life before she came to the city. "All those lake towns are pretty much the same."

They were quiet a while, then Lily said, "What's up? Do you guys have something on my client?"

He squinted into the sun before pulling a pair of sunglasses from the windshield. Okay, so she was under the impression that this was work related.

"Nope. Just a pleasure cruise. I was about to head out when you texted and figured you could use some time on the water as much as me." Maybe that would make it clearer to her that this was a date. "I thought we'd dock at Sinbad's and grab dinner in a while." There. That should leave no doubt.

"Am I dressed for it?"

"Yes, they get lots of boaters, even those coming in from the lakes. And in case you didn't notice, I'm wearing board shorts."

"I noticed. It's a little odd to see you out of your suit and tie. Dinner after a cruise down the river sounds great."

He could tell she was holding something back, but he focused on navigating the water. She'd get to what she wanted to say eventually. She always did. But then the silence went on for too long, and he asked if she was okay.

"Sure," she said.

"Did you go see that therapist on Monday? I thought about you on Sunday and hoped you'd keep your appointment."

"Sunday was hard, but yes, I saw Dr. Cam on Monday. Every day I get a little further from the shock of seeing people shot in front of me. You'll be happy to know my therapist assures me the panic was normal and my PTR, Post Traumatic Recovery, is intact."

He was sure there was more to it, but he didn't say anything. At least she'd kept her appointment. While at first he thought he had been confusing his feelings of protectiveness for her with his guilt about Trevor, now he felt if it ever was that, it had changed into something else. He liked her. She had guts, and she was gorgeous. He wanted her to be well for her own sake. He wanted to be with her for his.

After they passed the riverfront park and Victory Motors, he looped around and headed upriver past Chene Park with the canvas rooftop that looked like it would blow over in a good storm. He found the little nook he liked to stop in just before the big mansions on Jefferson came into view.

"We'll just stay here for a bit." He cut the engine, and the fine boat bobbed easily on the chop. "It's a party on the lake every day up a mile or two." There was barely another boat where they were. Everyone liked to head out to little swim islands on Lake St. Clair.

"For what it's worth, I checked out Jimmy's opera story. He was there."

Paxton sighed. Work again.

"His financials check out?"

"So far."

"I get it that the opera thing was a waste of time. I know if he hired Bingo, it doesn't matter if he was at the opera or in Katmandu. I'm humoring him. He wants me to believe him. He's paying me." Lily stood, grabbing the windshield to get her sea legs. The patina of the wood on the boat gleamed in the sun. "The wood on the bow of the boat is the exact color of your eyes. Like tea. Usually black men have much darker eyes."

"Thanks." Women loved his eyes. Even when he was a boy. It seemed like an improvement over work talk. "Most black folks have some white in them, going way back." He wondered if she knew what he meant.

"You mean because slave owners raped the women."

He didn't think she'd be so open about that, but she kept talking.

"I took a black history class in college. I think I was the only white person in that class," she said. "I had a huge crush on Toni Morrison, and after I read *Beloved* in lit class, I decided to learn more. Study up. It was stupid for me to mention your eyes."

"I like your eyes, too. And your hair. And your sassy mouth. I never know what you're going to say next." He turned slightly toward Lily, checking her out, seeing if something in her body language would tell him what was what.

She brought up how Jimmy had sworn he thought the stalker was his brother Dan. "That was before we caught Bingo," she said.

He smiled and tried not to laugh at the "we." "Jimmy's made excuses for that kid and pulled him out of scrapes his entire life. That kind of family dynamic doesn't shift," Paxton said. "And your eyes are the color of the sky just before it's about to storm."

They'd been gazing easily at each other, but when he talked about her eyes, she looked down. She had a smile on her face.

"We're on a date, right?" Lily said.

"Yes. You good with that?"

"I am. Just sort of surprised. I mean, I could tell we were getting to be friendly."

"I don't date much, and I'm thinking you don't either. Half of what we say to each other is about the case. But there's more, I think. I guess if we see each other socially, we'll find out."

She nodded. "I have a confession to make."

"What?"

"I don't do well with relationships with men."

"Welcome to the club. I have an ex-wife." Paxton might as well tell her a few pertinent details.

"Ouch."

"It wasn't a long marriage. Less than two years."

"So who broke up with whom?"

"Oh, the first time it was her. The second time it was me."

"Complicated. I get that. For me, since I moved to Detroit, it's just been easier not to have any relationships: no family, no friends, no lovers. Uncomplicated."

The hot sun was beating down into the boat, glinting off the water. Paxton felt a little bit like he was in hot water. He started up the boat to get the air moving again. Let them both cool down a bit. Let the conversation slow for now. He'd forgotten how women always wanted to talk out their feelings. He saw the open water ahead and sped up until it felt like the boat was barely skimming the waves.

They didn't say anything, both of them cooling off and enjoying it. Well, he hoped she was enjoying it.

"I have one more confession to make," she said as they pulled into a slip at Sinbad's.

"What's that?" He did a quick little sequence to tie up the boat without her help, then reached out to help her onto the dock.

"It's a bit long, and it's a work thing, so I'll tell it over dinner, if that's okay."

"Sure. But this is an active case, and your client is a person of interest, so don't be pissed if I can't answer a question."

"It's not a question. It's a request. Well, first let me tell you what I found out, and then you can decide if the request is legit."

"Deal."

They were early, and it was a weeknight, so they were quickly seated and served. Paxton noticed Lily waited for the wine to arrive, waited until she'd had a long sip, before she started telling him about her attempt to locate Eban Stern. She went through meeting Melanie, which of course he knew because he'd been there at Kennedy's funeral, but she gave the particulars of their conversation or at least the parts that were relevant to Eban Stern. By the time she finished, she'd drained her glass of wine and the server had taken their dinner order.

"At first, I thought it was just a matter of tracking him down, but it feels like a skip. Don't you think?"

"Maybe. What's your request?"

"Well...I can't subpoena disconnected phone

records, but you can. If you think there's anything here."

"And with the phone records, you could check all the numbers he called more than once. And then call those numbers and ask if they had his new phone number or if they knew his address."

"Yes. Or I could go through every Stern in the phone book. If you still think my client is the only possible person who could have hired Bingo."

"He's still the only one with a motive."

"True. But…" She stopped talking and was looking toward the front of the restaurant.

"What?" Paxton said.

"I think that's the chief of police. And he's heading our way."

Paxton turned. His mother and father. His sisters. His niece.

"It's fine," he said to Lily, just before his mother reached their table and bent to kiss his cheek.

"Hello, darling," she said.

Paxton got up and moved next to Lily. "Hi Mama. Dad. Everybody." He touched Lily gently on the shoulder. "This is Lily. She's the PI who shot that video that led to the arrest of the hit man in the double homicide last weekend. Lily, meet the family." He rattled off his sisters' names and Star's. Star was staring at Lily.

"Is she your girlfriend, Uncle Paxton?"

Star was six, and she didn't have any filters.

"Yes, Star. This is Lily White. Lily, this is little Star."

Star giggled and smacked her hand on her forehead. "Your name is White, and you are white!"

she said.

Lily chuckled. "That's true. And your name is Star, and you twinkle."

Star smiled widely. His mother took over the conversations. "When you called to say you were taking the boat out, we just figured you'd stop in here for dinner. We didn't know you had a date."

"It's fine," Lily said at the same time Paxton said the same thing. He noticed that she didn't deny they were on a date.

"Chief Paxton," his dad said, holding out his hand to Lily. "Good to meet you, Ms. White. I wanted to thank you personally for your service to the department. My son is very impressed with your skills."

One of his sisters let out a short laugh; he bet it was Estella. His mother said, "Hush." Star held her hand over her mouth, the movement of her shoulders clearly indicating her glee in catching her uncle with a woman. The first any of them had met since his divorce.

Lily stood and shook Dad's proffered hand. "It's an honor to meet you, Chief."

They shook hands, and then Dad said, "Sit, sit." Which was good because the server was standing with their dinner plates in his hands. The family made way.

"Well," his dad said, "we can see you're not having another solo dinner, so we'll leave you two to your meal."

His family followed a hostess to a large round table not quite far enough away for Paxton's comfort.

"They seem nice," Lily said.

"I'm sorry about that," Paxton said.

"No, don't be. I mean, I hope it's not awkward for you."

Paxton was not about to spoil the meal by telling Lily that word had gotten around about her part in Bingo's arrest and nobody was going easy on him. All good-natured ribbing about how he'd suddenly picked up not just Bill Nigel, a white partner, but another sort of white partner, too. He ignored everyone, but he was sure his dad had heard the gossip by now. Not that he would do or say anything about any of it unless somehow somebody made a case that it could be a conflict of interest to date the PI whose current client was the guy the department was very busy building a case against.

They ate in silence for a while, then Lily said, "I'm not great at small talk. That's why I like talking to you. We can talk about work. I really don't want to talk about politics or religion or what black person got shot in the back by a white cop this week…"

"I know." The way her voice got quieter when she commented on the long-running shooting of black men by white cops showed she had empathy for his people. That was enough for now to quell any uneasiness he'd had about seeing a white woman.

They were silent for a bit as he searched for a new topic. He had not listened to any new music in ten years, so there went that. She probably didn't like sports, and he didn't go to movies. Damn, he was boring. "I'm fine talking shop. Have you thought about Eban Stern's motive?" There. Safe ground. Plus she smiled at him with what he hoped was gratitude. Couple of workaholics. Deserved each other. Now he was smiling like an idiot too.

"No. I can't think of anything. In fact, just the opposite. Maybe he got freaked out by the murders of two of his co-workers and split town."

"But that *is* weird about his address being false."

"Yep. Anybody can disconnect a cell phone for a thousand reasons, but not so much that."

"It's the only thing that makes me want to check. I can't subpoena the records yet. There's not enough there. But I can find out if it was a disposable."

"But then again, lots of people use disposable cell phones. I mean, he could be trying to avoid paying child support."

"I guess you see a lot of that."

"And then sometimes it's a crazy ex-girlfriend thing. I've learned to spot those."

She talked a little bit about the woman who had hired her to find a "lost love" on an early case. Turns out the lover had gotten lost on purpose. Lily let him stay gone and had told the woman he couldn't be reached. "Which was true. He couldn't be reached by her because I was not about to divulge his whereabouts."

Paxton laughed. "Good call."

"Yeah, so with this, I'm not feeling like Jimmy did it. I don't like his brother for it either. Just in case your mind is moving that way." She told Paxton her theory about Danny which pretty much went why carry a romantic burning torch from afar for so many years and then turn around and become pathologically jealous enough, and organized enough, to hire not just one kill, but two?

She made good points, but so far the clearest motive was still held by her client Jimmy Heyl.

"What made you think about Eban Stern for hiring the murders in the first place?"

"It kind of started with Kennedy. He told me about a top-secret work project he and Roseann were working on with Melanie and Eban, trying to track down a hacker into Victory's system. Kennedy said they thought it was an inside job...didn't I tell you all this?"

"Yeah," he admitted. "I just like hearing you think out loud."

"Okay, well, here's something I didn't tell you. Melanie said the whole secret hacker thing turned out to be some kind of error in the system. Which again makes Stern an unlikelier suspect than I first thought. I'm just at the point where I'm crossing people off the list."

"Just be careful," he said.

"I always am. You having dessert?"

Paxton couldn't help but be aware of his family seated a little too close for comfort, but he tried not to show it. And failed.

"No. Forget it. Your peeps are probably checking us out and speculating and so forth."

Lily and Star had exchanged two or three waves so far. The rest of the clan was politely pretending they weren't within shouting distance.

"We could take the boat back to the Yacht Club and go somewhere from there."

"Sounds like a plan," Lily said.

She excused herself, saying she wanted to stop in the powder room, so he said he'd meet her after he took care of the check. While he signed, she walked over to say goodbye to his family. She gave Star a hug and exchanged a few words with Star's mother, his sister, LaDonna. She left without looking back at him. Now every single one of his closest relatives, not one of them trying to hide it, stared right at him. At least half of them were grinning. He went over to say his goodbyes, wondering if Lily liked ice cream or pie or, his preference, one on top of the other.

Chapter 11

Lily

I didn't blame Paxton for refusing, in the nicest way possible, to subpoena Eban Stern's telephone records. After we'd talked about it and tossed around all the various reasons why Stern might want to skip town, I understood why Paxton still thought my client was the guy behind the murders. Also he'd been very sweet and bought me pie and ice cream after we'd docked the boat, but Paxton got a text during dessert, stopped eating, seemed preoccupied. He dropped me off at my vehicle still parked on Belle Isle and must have forgotten we'd had a date, because he didn't even try to kiss me.

Fine. Today, it was back to work. I drank my coffee at the little table by the window, finally opening up my laptop and viewing the overwhelming listings for people with the last name of Stern in the Metro Detroit area. If only I knew where to start. Was he even from the Detroit area or had he moved here from another state? Or upstate?

Melanie might know. And I was supposed to call her today. Arrange lunch. Lunch in the West Village would be something to look forward to after hours of cold calling people named Stern and asking if they were related to Eban. Why, if Paxton and I had decided Stern had no motive for murdering his co-workers, was I even doing this? Maybe I should go right on to Danny Heyl, next on my list of unlikely but possible mental cases with psychopathic tendencies who had hired two people's deaths.

Instead, I finished my coffee and mentally prepared to make the calls. I didn't like this part of the job, but I liked to close loops. Eban Stern was an open loop. I called Melanie. Who sounded really happy to hear from me. We made a plan to meet for lunch the next day. Before we hung up, I asked her if Stern had ever mentioned where he grew up.

"Hmmm. We really weren't that close. We had coffee once or twice at the beginning of the project, though."

I waited for Melanie to think back, to remember, even while I admitted to myself that if he had grown up in Metro Detroit, that didn't mean his family still lived in the same community. But I had to start somewhere.

"I don't know. I think Bloomfield Hills, but I'm not sure. Sorry."

"Bloomfield Hills. Okay, that's great. Thanks."

"Did you get him on his cell phone yesterday?"

"No. Disconnected."

"He was probably freaked out about two of our team being killed. I guess he didn't stick around to find out that the killer is in jail."

"Yeah, he probably just freaked out and split." I stopped a beat. "Are you okay?"

"Well, I'm not scared. Just—it hurts. I miss Tom in a bad way. I knew I loved him. I just didn't know how much. So I'm grieving, and that's going to be true for a long time. But, you know, the husband, your client, he thought Roseann and Tom were having an affair. That's what the newspapers say. If Eban hadn't quit so quick, he could have read that for himself."

I wondered if Melanie remembered that as "the husband" was my client, I was trying to clear him, trying to find out who else might have hired the hits. But she was pregnant and beyond sad, and so I didn't want to remind her of these stark facts.

"You're right. I want to speak to him, though, just to cross him off my list."

"List?"

"Suspects. I'll tell you about it at lunch tomorrow," I promised.

The listings for Stern in Bloomfield Hills were significantly fewer than the entire greater Detroit area. I'd start there and spread out to the bordering cities, and then the cities that bordered those. I was very glad the new phones had built-in voice commands. I didn't have to punch in all those numbers. All I had to do was tell the phone to do it. Then talk.

And talk I did, asking the same question the same way to the same answer for a couple of hours. The question was "Are you a relative of Eban Stern?" and the answer was always a variation of "No." Some people said it and cut me off without a goodbye. Some people wanted to know how I'd gotten their number. Some people told me they had a son named Evan or a cousin named Abe, so there were a few instances of spelling out E-B-A-N. Two guys asked me if I was single. I hung up on them.

By eleven o'clock, I'd finished the pot of coffee room service had delivered that morning. I ate a banana from the fruit bowl housekeeping replenished every week and stretched out my back and neck with a little light yoga. I checked the clock. Okay, thirty more minutes, ten or fifteen more calls, and then I'd be done and could move on to Dan Heyl.

The sixth call into my second round was a little weird. I asked my standard question ("Is Eban there?"), but the woman who answered the phone said, "Who wants to know?" Her voice suggested she was in a bad mood. Or maybe she was a suspicious girlfriend.

"I'm sorry!" I said. "I should have introduced myself. I used to work with Eban at Victory Motors, and I wanted to return the twenty dollars he lent me a few weeks ago."

"You have the wrong number."

"Oh, sorry." I didn't know if that was true or not. I made a note of the name and number. I didn't quite close my loop, but I'd check into Claire Stern's background a little deeper. After I went to see Dan Heyl.

****

Dan Heyl didn't look anything like Jimmy. Long hair, skinny as a lizard, eyes clouded. From the smell of him, the weed he'd been smoking was homegrown. Dan's bar, Coda, was not what I expected, either. Instead of tasteful, it was pastiche. Dark and light wood mixed freely with stainless steel bar stools, an enormous amateur photo montage on one wall, more random than studied, juxtaposed with a pool table at the other end of the room. Dozens of dusty baseball trophies lined up above the liquor bottles at the bar that ran a line down the center of the place. He was going for cool classic Cass Corridor, but the place just ended up looking run-down and weird.

I recognized Dan from when Jimmy had introduced us at Roseann's funeral, so I took a seat at the bar he stood behind and ordered a Chardonnay. Was a tad early in the day, but when I sit at a bar, I drink. It's a reflex. Dan poured a healthy glass of house wine.

If I could eliminate both Jimmy and Dan as suspects, then somehow tie Eban Stern to Bingo, Paxton would no longer be able to ignore my theory that the two crimes were related. At least that was the working plan. Jimmy had told me he'd do whatever he could to help his brother.

"Dan, my man," a guy in a motorcycle jacket and thick-soled black boots yelled. "Two more." The guy sitting next to him, also in leathers, even though it was a hot summer day, was junkie thin. "And put on the television, would ya?"

The clientele was not what one would expect in Grosse Pointe, either. Besides the two jokers one stool down from me, a couple made illicit eyes at each other in a booth adjacent to the bar. Then there was me, day drinking. But I didn't have anything planned, other than following up the thin lead of Claire Stern for a possible connection to Eban, so I cut myself a break. I looked around again in case I'd missed another patron or two, perhaps lurking in a dark corner or just returning from the restrooms, but the rest of the bar stools and booths were empty.

Jimmy had called me early in the morning, yelling that the Detroit PD was ready to hang Roseann and Kennedy's deaths on Dan because they had no better suspects. "And your guy Paxton is key on the case," Jimmy had added. I wondered if that had something to do with the text Paxton had gotten during dessert last night.

Meanwhile, Eban Stern had vanished off the face of the planet. At least he was not in any hotel in Detroit or the metro area. He had not used a credit card in the past seventy-two hours. His phone was disconnected, and his personal history, such as it was, had been purged from Victory's database before he left the company. All of this did not add up to a motive, except maybe Stern being motivated by fear of a psycho-hacker to get out of town and clear any trail he'd left behind.

Dan poured beers, measured shots, turned on the television. And there was Paxton and his dad, up on the screen. The press conference. I wasn't sure what Jimmy had told Dan about my relationship with Paxton—I wasn't sure how much Jimmy actually knew about it himself. Just then, Dan turned to me and said, "That the guy you're banging?"

"What? Wait. You say she's doing a—" the biker in boots yelled.

I shot out of my seat and onto Boots, knocking over the stool between us. I shoved my arm across his mouth before he could finish his sentence. "Shut up," I said, noticing I'd also stepped on his steel toes. Before he could bite me, I sat back down.

Paxton and I weren't as far along in our relationship as Dan-via-Jimmy seemed to think. Still, I wasn't going to have any asshole spewing racial slurs in front of me. The chief spoke into a microphone as Paxton stood a step behind him in front of headquarters.

Even the couple who only had eyes for each other were looking at the television now. I wondered how many people here knew, besides Dan and me, that the "second suspect in the double homicide we are very close to arresting" might just be the guy pouring our booze.

Boots and Skinny weren't wearing colors, but they had that look about them, like they were dangerous characters and wanted everyone to know it. They kept shooting me dirty looks but so far hadn't said anything else to me. And yet, assholes, I had learned, could sometimes be dangerous. Still, if they'd left their colors in the parking lot, they'd left their weapons there, too. This place must have been crawling with cops in the last few days, perhaps one reason for the dearth of customers. I flipped open my purse with an eye toward arming myself then and there. But before I could pull a weapon part way out of my purse to at least let them have a look at it, Boots and Skinny threw down their sweaty dollars and booked.

I was happy to see them go. Dan flicked off the television. The oblivious lovers in the booth went back to touching each other inappropriately.

"You gotta come back at night," Dan said to me.

"Because?" I nodded when he lifted the bottle of wine to the rim of my empty glass. He filled it.

"Things change around here. That's when I make my money. The bands are top shelf. The booze, not so much. Listen, babe, my brother told me you'd help me out here. My books don't balance because I've got a sideline in medical marijuana." He paused, then added, "Not strictly legal. Sometimes my bank balance is too high and sometimes it's too low."

I shrugged and sipped my wine. "That's too bad. I'd like to help, but I got nowhere to go with this unless you can help me out. Like, something on Bingo? Heard you knew him." I hadn't heard any such thing, but it was worth a shot.

"I don't know that hit man, okay? Everybody keeps asking me that. He was a friend of a friend."

"You ever hear of Eban Stern?"

"No, why?"

"No reason." Fishing expeditions mostly came up empty, but I had to try.

"Is he your suspect? I hope so. I hope you find him. I have a medical condition. I need my treatment, and I won't get herb inside."

We'd both heard what the chief had said about an arrest being imminent. They had nothing on Dan, but with his messed-up bank records, they could still try to pin conspiracy to commit murder on Dan despite his motive being weak. Dan had had an incurable crush on Roseann since they were in high school. Why would he want to hire a guy to murder her now? I looked at the lovers in the booth, now arguing bitterly. The cops were right about one thing. Love was almost as good a motive for murder as money. I had to admit it was possible. Dan could be my man in this scam.

I took the gun out of my purse and stuck it discreetly into the rear waistband of my jeans before I went into the parking lot. No sign of Boots and Skinny or their bikes. I eased my weapon out of my pants and onto my lap as I sat behind the wheel. Why take chances with those racist shitheads?

I was stopped at a light on Mack when I spotted the bikers. There were four of them, two to a lane, on my immediate right. I was checking them out to see if I could make Boots and Skinny, which is why I missed the guy on my right who opened my passenger door with a crowbar.

I jerked at the unexpected noise, and my weapon fell between the gas pedal and the brake. I went to reach for it, but the guy used the crowbar to jerk my arm up while he jumped into the passenger seat. He jammed a gun to my head and told me to drive. He cocked the cheap revolver and bent down to retrieve my gun. I prayed the weapon wouldn't go off, sat very still, and did his bidding.

As I threaded my way out of Grosse Pointe and into Detroit, I felt sure somebody would notice a woman being held at gunpoint as she drove through the city's east side, but no. I was on the verge of panic, but I held my shit together by sheer willpower. It was do this or die, and I didn't feel like dying today. Somewhere near Brush Park, he moved the gun from my head to my gut and told me to pull over. I stole a quick glance at him, thin with a bowling ball paunch. Dark greasy clumps made it hard to say if his hair was blond or brown. His eyes twitched when they caught mine, and he shoved the gun an inch further into my rib cage.

"Take a picture, it will last longer than your life."

I moved my eyes off his face. I hate when assholes hold all the aces.

"Open the door on your side."

Before I could do that, the window smashed, the door swung open, and I fell into a black hole.

Chapter 12

Paxton

Paxton knew Lily had probably seen the press conference by now. She wasn't answering her phone, was probably upset about that "imminent arrest" bullshit his dad had read off to the media. He wanted to tell her it was unlikely her client would be arrested. More likely his brother would be going down for the crime. The kid's financials were being worked over and while there were no direct ties to Bingo, there'd been several small withdrawals in the same time frame as Bingo claimed he'd gotten paid. Bingo had also said he knew Dan, although he'd identified three different voices as the one he'd made the plan with, and none of those voices had been Dan Heyl's.

Paxton had been home for a couple of hours debating calling Lily. He really didn't have a reason, except that he wanted to hear her voice. So far, all he'd gotten was her voice on a recorded message. He decided to head over to the casino.

If she was home, she wasn't answering her door. That would be a first. He went down to the hotel check-in desk. The guy running the desk said he hadn't seen Lily. He'd come on duty at six o'clock.

"Who worked the day shift?"

"Lorene."

Paxton knew Lorene. She was friendly with Lily. She also liked to gamble her paycheck away. Paxton walked down the long corridor that led to the casino. He could smell the smoke from a hundred feet. Over in the Windsor, just across the bridge, they didn't let anybody smoke in the casino. In Detroit, a casino was about the only public place you could smoke.

The smoke, the noise. Didn't know how people actually enjoyed losing their paycheck in these places. But he made his way around the slot machines where people pressed buttons like automatons. Pretty soon they'd have something where you blinked your eyes to turn the wheel. Hands free. He passed the stage where bands from the 80s, once selling out arenas, came to sing their old songs. Finally, he spotted Lorene playing blackjack.

"Hey, Lorene."

"Hey." She looked somewhat distrustful, as most people did when he entered into their dens of iniquity.

"I was looking for Lily. You see her today?"

"She helping you on a case, right?" Just the mention of Lily's name made Lorene smile.

He smiled and nodded slightly. Lily had helped him.

"She went out around lunch time. I didn't see her come home."

Home. Funny place to call a casino hotel, but it seemed to work for Lily. She must be working a new case. There's no way she'd be interviewing Dan Heyl all day and all night. Unless. Hell. Maybe she liked Dan. Maybe they struck up some kind of something. No. Guy was a pothead. Lily was smarter than that.

He shook his head to get the image of Lily with

another guy out of his head. "Thanks, Lorene." He started to walk away. He was an idiot. Lily was a free agent. Hell, he hadn't even kissed her last night. He thought about her lips, plump and red from the cherry pie. Yep. Idiot.

He found himself driving down Jefferson and into Grosse Pointe. Dan's bar. They'd brought him in. He'd made a statement. They had his financials, personal and business. Unfortunately for Dan, especially if he was innocent, he also had small payments come to him through Diablo's check-cashing racket. That was the trick that tightened the knot in the rope around Dan's neck. Until they had an arrest warrant in place, there was nothing left to say to the guy. Except to ask if he'd seen Lily today.

The bar smelled like weed, but Paxton didn't give a shit. Lily had left a little after two that afternoon, Heyl said. "She's on the case. Trying to prove my innocence." The guy was stoned. He told some story about how Lily pulled out a gun on some biker guys who had made a crack about Paxton and Lily going out. "They don't like black on white, man. Me, I'm cool with it."

Paxton didn't bother to reply. When Heyl pointed out the bikers who Lily had had words with, Paxton didn't bother to question them. If they had Lily, they wouldn't be here.

He went home. Lily was a big girl. She could take care of herself.

The next day, he did his job. He didn't call Lily. Why should he? There was nothing new on the case, no reason to call her, and he tried really hard to think of one. Thoughts of her kept interfering with work. He pushed them aside. Why was he even thinking about her? He must have it bad. He'd dreamed about her last night. He thought about her, some silly thing she said, and he'd smile.

He had to admit it. It was pretty plain. It was pretty simple. He had it bad for her. And she was slightly messed up. She had that PTSD—damn, she said she was in recovery but didn't recovery last all the rest of your life? Wasn't she damaged beyond what he was comfortable with, if, hypothetically, they did end up together? Damn, he hadn't had a relationship in a long time. Hadn't wanted one. Didn't want one now. But still. She'd taken up residence in his head.

He went back to the report he was reading for Nigel. Guy was working out great, but they'd reached a dead space. Nigel was wringing everything he could for the arrest warrant of Dan Heyl. Nothing fit as neatly as it needed to. Didn't feel right, either. Paxton read the same sentence three times. He was very happy when the phone rang.

"Hi, is this Detective Paxton?"

He asked who wanted to know. The woman had called his direct line. And she wasn't Lily.

"This is a friend of Lily's. You gave me your number—I worked with Thomas Kennedy and Roseann Heyl."

"Oh, right. Melanie. What's up?"

"I don't know. Lily was supposed to be here for lunch an hour ago. I just wondered if you knew where she was. She's not answering her phone, and the front desk at her hotel said she hasn't been around. She gets coffee delivered every morning, but today nobody answered."

Not good. "Maybe she met someone? Went home with him?"

Melanie snorted. "You know her, right? She told me you were her only friend, and she doesn't seem like the type to go one-night-wild."

"What about you? You're having lunch, right? So you're also her friend."

"We're just getting to know each other. I was helping her with Eban Stern. She wanted to close the loop on him, or something like that."

"I'm sorry she stood you up, Melanie. It's not like her. She may have been unavoidably detained."

"I was thinking the same thing. But she told me you two were tight, and Lorene, the girl on the desk at the hotel, said you'd been checking on her last night, and nobody over there has seen her or heard from her in like twenty-four hours. I'm a little worried. I mean, she said the guy who killed my co-workers is in jail, but someone, like Roseann's husband, right? Somebody hired this guy. So maybe, I don't know. I'm being silly, maybe?"

"No, not at all. You're right. It's not like Lily to be out of touch like this. But maybe she got another case. She could have had to go out of town."

"But she'd at least text me. She's not rude. She wouldn't just not show up like that."

"Well, I'll look into it, okay? Don't worry. She's fine. It's possible lunch just slipped her mind."

"I don't think so. Will you tell her to call me if you find her?"

"Of course. I'm sure there's a logical explanation for everything."

Paxton hoped what he said was true, but he had a bad feeling he couldn't shake.

Chapter 13

Lily

I came to consciousness in layers; the painful bump on the left side of my head helped me to piece things together. The smashing of my car window had come via blunt force from the same object that then must have been applied to my hard head. After carefully fingering my throbbing, stinging injury, matted with what I suspected was dried blood, I opened my eyes.

My childhood bedroom. Okay, this was a nightmare. I was lying down in a bed. Being asleep was the only scenario that made sense in the moment. I did the thing where I told myself, "This is a dream," to snap myself out of sleep, but it didn't work. I wasn't waking up. Not even after I pinched myself.

I got out of bed, went into the bathroom. Nothing in here was the same as my childhood bathroom at all. Sink, toilet, no shower. Cement floor. Raw wood on the walls. No closet, no tub, no spa products. Not even a hairbrush. Not even a mirror. I went back into the bedroom. It looked the same as my childhood furniture. I tried the desk drawer. It stuck the same as mine had. Except it was empty. I checked the dresser drawers, all six of them. They were empty too.

And the floor. It wasn't my floor. It was concrete. Plus this room had no windows like my childhood room. I went to the door—it wasn't my door—and pulled it open. Bars behind the door, like a jail cell. A cement room like a basement with a bare light bulb outside the bars. Yes, this was my bed, my dresser, even my matching desk, but everything else was different. My bed didn't even have a sheet on it, not a blanket or a pillow. On the plus side, there was no blood from my head wound on the mattress. On the other side, I had to hope there was no internal bleeding.

I left the door open to the cell bars and looked up. Whoever had put me here had gone to the trouble to do one of those tile ceilings. It did not extend to the room outside my cell. I went back into the bathroom. At the sink, I wet a lone washcloth and eased it over the bloody aching lump on my head. Where was my purse? My set of pick locks? My meds? My gun? All of it, I supposed, in custody of the squirrely greasy guy with the twitch in his eye.

My body started to clamor for benzos. My heartbeat increased with every deep breath. I felt dizzy and lay down on the stripped bed, still holding the cool cloth to my head. I couldn't stop my heartbeats from ticking past anxiety into panic. I imagined somebody had a tiny camera in the ceiling tiles and was watching me. Just in case someone was watching remotely, I tried to appear unfazed despite sheer dread. *Stop it. Breath. You won't die. Not from panic, anyway.* Hours or minutes passed in this way. I had no watch, no clock, no phone. My head hurt, my jaw had frozen in perma-tense, my eyes burned, every muscle in my body ached.

Most of these physical symptoms were my own fault. I'd been leaning too hard on meds again since the murders, and now the lack of it was paying me back with withdrawal symptoms. On the positive side, if I was in withdrawal, that meant at least twenty-four hours had passed since my last dose. I hadn't taken anything the day I went to see Dan Heyl. I'd left Coda about one in the afternoon, so it must now be the next day, noon or maybe later. Calculating that kept my mind off the withdrawals for entire seconds at a time.

I needed water, but when I gingerly paced to the bathroom again, there was no glass. Of course not. That would make it too easy to escape my captors by slitting my wrists. Which I'd never do, but whoever was holding me in this bizarre cell didn't know that. Who were those fuckers, and what did they want with me? I cupped my hand, but it trembled too much to drink from so I bent over and put my mouth to the faucet. My lips were so dry. I needed lip balm. Christ. Once I got out of here, I'd break my dependence on pills and goddamn lip gloss.

I checked every inch of wall and floor for an escape. Checked the ceiling tiles for a mini-cam or a clue. Nothing. No sounds but my own breathing. I went through everything in my tiny prison, turning over how anything might be used as a pick lock. The desk and dresser drawers were the only options, although wood splinters were not ideal. Not even useful unless I wanted to stick them under my fingernails to jolt my stomach out of the knot it was tied in. My head pulsed, like a stab to the brain, over and over again. Ignore it. What could I do with this hardware, tiny screws and curlicue fake French drawer pulls? Not a damn thing except break my fingernails, I quickly discovered.

Eventually, someone would come. Maybe. Unless they meant to starve me. My stomach growled. I ignored it and considered who "they" were, coming to the rapid conclusion that "they" could only be one person: my father. My only living relative. He was the only person who could possibly have saved my childhood furniture. But why? As simple as payback because I'd sent him to prison? Maybe, but it seemed like a lot of trouble without much payoff. Who else had reason to hurt me? Bingo, but he'd just shoot me, and anyway he was in jail. Eban Stern? His hypothetical girlfriend Claire? Maybe Stern would get into my laptop and blow it up, which would almost kill me, but I didn't see someone obsessed by computer code planning a real-life elaborate mind game. I still couldn't shake the firm idea that somehow Papa was behind this. But was it connected to my case? How could it be?

What had Dan said? Bingo had been in a cush prison "for a minute" before he got sent to Jackson. So what if Bingo had been sent to my dad's cozy rehabilitation facility for the rich? Papa had ended up there because he was some kind of big shot in business and our family had money. Also his lawyer made a big to-do about that video I shot. And he had a point. I did entrap Papa into confessing. I did put that video on YouTube before anyone could stop me. I did cause the jury to be prejudiced. At the time, I hadn't known how else to be sure my father would rot in prison.

Papa, not Dan, might just be the guy who hired Bingo. But why? To frame my client? To make me look incompetent? That seemed like a whole lot of trouble to go through to teach me a lesson. And what about Twitch Eye and his head-bashing accomplice? There was more to this than I'd even conceived. How did Papa arrange it from prison? My head throbbed, and I fell into a fitful sleep.

I woke and didn't know if it was day or night. The single light bulb was still burning, and the rooms contained no switch to turn it off or on. That was okay. I'd rather it be left on. I couldn't see any windows inside or outside my cell, so if my captor wanted to, he could keep me in darkness. My anxiety had skyrocketed at the thought, but that was probably just another withdrawal symptom from the meds.

Knowing something is a withdrawal symptom doesn't make it go away. I got up, felt dizzy, sat again. I probably had a concussion. Or maybe I was just hungry. I decided to walk the perimeter of the small cell just for something to do. I'd count the steps. That would take my mind off the anxiety, the end-of-the-world scenario, the torture and rape scenario. It was likely the world would not end today. It was possible I'd be raped and even tortured, but would Papa go that far? Even with the anxiety kicking up a notch, I didn't believe he'd hire somebody to do that.

I counted something like twelve thousand steps when I lost track and gave up. My legs were tired. My head hurt. I slept again. Woke again. Had I been here one day? Two? Did anybody miss me? I'd had a lunch date with Melanie. She probably just figured I'd flaked. Would Paxton miss me? I don't know why he should. Yes, he was nice to me, but he hadn't even tried to kiss me after our date. So it couldn't have been a date. Because if it was a date, there would be a kiss. Unless he decided he didn't like me after all. My stomach grumbled. My head throbbed. I wanted some cherry pie. I wanted coffee. I wanted out of here.

Try as I might, I could not work out how or why

Papa would want to kill my client's wife. And her co-worker. It was stupid, really. And I wasn't even sure he knew Bingo, if they'd been incarcerated together. I couldn't find out for sure until I got out of this hell hole. Or. Did he intend for me to never get out? Was Twitch Eye simply to leave me here to die of dehydration?

Damn that dad of mine. I'd wanted to leave my past behind, but he wouldn't let me. Well, if I ever got out of here alive, I'd go right to his stupid prison and I'd confront him. With what? No, maybe I'd go straight to Paxton and tell him my theory and then…but Paxton didn't like my theories. For all I knew, Dan Heyl was in jail right now. How in the world did Papa pull this off from inside a prison cell? If he could do that from his cell, I should be able to do something from mine.

Minutes or hours went by. I knew how to meditate because that was part of my recovery, so I kept trying to make my mind like an empty rice bowl. When thoughts came up, which they do about every three seconds, I noticed them and let them drift away. I've heard of these meditation retreats where people go to meditate for an entire weekend. They don't speak or even make eye contact with anyone else. I'd always thought I'd never be able to do that, and maybe it's karma for killing a man, but I was in a kind of forced retreat right now.

I hated thinking about my cousin. I'd been obsessed over the damage he'd done, but I'd finally been able to release it. I knew I had had no choice but to kill him. I'd made my peace. Or so I thought. I was sick of my thoughts but couldn't keep them away. I saw how it must be for people in solitary confinement, who could go insane. I wasn't insane yet, but I hadn't been here that long. Two days? Four? More?

Nothing changed for a long time, then the scent of those Detroit burger sliders I'd become semi-addicted to met my nostrils. Someone must be coming. I thought furiously as I salivated at the smell of cheap grilled meat. Twitch Eye turned a corner into view a bag of food tucked under the arm of his dirty, and possibly sweaty, arm, which effectively killed my appetite. I tensed, ready for what came next.

He plucked a key from his pocket, fit it into the lock, twisted it, opened the hinge. I lunged. Twitch Eye fell as the heavy door slammed open on him. I ran for the place where I'd been imagining steps, ran up them and through an open door. I was in some kind of shop. Old, musty smelling, shelves full of books, lamps, dishes, an ancient cash register. I ran past it all in a blur, toward the light coming in from a dirty window. I heard him yelling, swearing, calling out to someone else. There was the door. I opened it and ran out into the street.

Detroit was a big city, and I wasn't familiar with this patch of grizzled turf, devoid of humanity, all crumbling cement, dirt and weeds. Any buildings except the one I'd been held in were either burned out or boarded up. The sun said it was high noon. I ran toward the alley, ducking into the dark corner behind a smelly Dumpster, hoping Twitch Eye hadn't seen me turn. He ran past me, disappeared from sight. I went the other way, into the street, and stuck out my thumb.

Two kids with letter jackets driving a sedan that probably belonged to their grandma stopped. I got in the back seat and bent my neck so they could see the blood on my head wound. "My boyfriend. He's trying to kill me," I said. "Can you take me to the police? I think he went the other way, but he might come back."

"Uh, you best get out," the passenger said. But the driver burned rubber. I kept my spinning head down and took deep breaths.

"Do you have a phone?"

The kid who'd wanted to dump me handed one over. I dialed Paxton with shaking fingers. "Thanks," I said, listening to Paxton's phone ring. "What day is it?"

Again, words and sounds that ran over me came from the front of the vehicle. "Paxton! Please pick up. I'm calling you right back. I'm in trouble. It's my dad."

"I thought you said it was your boyfriend?" The passenger's voice was becoming familiar to her. He sounded hostile. But the driver kept the car going. I only hoped it was heading toward a cop shop. Any cop shop.

"What city are we in? Detroit?"

"West side. Six Mile and McNichols."

Not downtown, but at least not Ohio. They'd driven maybe ten blocks.

"Can I have my phone back?" A hand tried to grab it, but I pulled my arm away, got up on the seat, pressed myself into the back seat cushion as far away as I could, hit redial.

Paxton answered. "Lily!" he shouted. "Are you okay? Where are you?"

Chapter 14

Paxton

Paxton sped down the Lodge toward the hospital. He parked at the emergency room doors, walked in brandishing his badge.

"Lily White?" He questioned the desk clerk without coming to a complete stop. She told him Lily's room number without mentioning his car was in a tow zone. A brisk walk and elevator ride brought him to her room.

"You came," she said when he entered.

He slowed, trying to stop the forward momentum that had propelled him since he'd gotten her call. "You're okay? They checked you over?"

"Yes. I'm fine. They did some kind of a scan. I have a concussion. I mean, I got it days ago so it must be getting better, but they insisted I stay the night. And everyone's freaking because I have no next of kin. Well, I do, but he's in jail. So that's why they called you."

"When you got cut off on the phone, the boys picked up and talked to me. I told them to bring you here. They said you blacked out?"

"I think I was just hungry."

He noticed the IV in her arm.

"Sit down," she said.

137

He looked at the chair. It was too far away. He sat on the bed.

"I'm sorry I didn't find you," he said. He was a cop. She was important to him. He had not known how important until she disappeared for three days. "At first, I thought you were working the case, but you've never been gone so long before. I kept trying your phone, and you didn't answer. I knew something was wrong. I called Jimmy, and he said you'd been to see his brother. Dan Heyl told me about your altercation with those bikers."

Heyl had repeated exactly what the racist dirt bags had started to say and how Lily stood up for him. He was not a guy to fall for just any girl, but when a tiny female steps on a big-ass biker's foot in your defense, well, something happens. Physically. His heart pried open. Painful and probably not smart, but Lily got to him.

"It wasn't the bikers. It was some twitch-eyed guy. And another person I didn't see."

"I've been in every MC in the city, hauled every single member down for questioning, including the two you mixed it up with. Zero leads."

He didn't say he'd been out of his mind with worry. He hadn't been able to eat or sleep. At first, he attributed these things to a work ethic taken too far, but in those early predawn hours trying to sleep and failing, he admitted it was more than work. He cared for Lily in a way he hadn't cared for a woman in a long time. It didn't help acknowledging his emotion. The rational part of his mind didn't think it at all wise to get too close. She was white. And a PI. She was relentless and reckless. But looking at her lying in the hospital bed, wearing one of those tissue-thin gowns with a pattern so faded it was hardly discernable, she just looked helpless. He was a goner.

"It's nothing to do with them. It's my dad." Lily rubbed her eye, causing the IV tube to yank her tender skin. He reached for her arm so she wouldn't pull the needle out, but his hand found her face. He brushed the hair hanging over her eyes back and trailed his knuckles down to graze her chin. Her hand found his, and she lowered her arm even as her fingers locked into his.

Lily told him the story about being knocked out cold and coming to in a room that looked exactly like her childhood bedroom. She'd been left alone, a prisoner in a basement of an abandoned consignment store, or maybe an antique store, on the far west side of the city. For three days.

"Okay, baby, take it easy," he said, worried about her physical and mental state. How had she coped? Were there internal injuries? Where was the doctor? Had he just called her "baby"? Christ.

"I'm fine, really," she said.

A doctor came in.

"You can tell him everything, doc. He's my…" Her words trailed off as she looked down at the bed, their hands still entwined on the blanket.

Paxton introduced himself.

The doctor listed the tests they'd run on Lily.

"She's a strong woman, Detective. Got a good crack on the head. Could have used stitches had we been there sooner. She's already started to heal, so we just bandaged her up good. The concussion didn't do any permanent damage. She was dehydrated but managed to take in a little water, which mitigated lack of food."

"When can she come home?" He wanted to ask about her PTSD and if they'd given her anything for the panic, but looking at her, she seemed unfazed. No signs of anxiety at all. Maybe they'd already sedated her.

"Well, we'd like to observe her overnight, just to be safe, but she should be fine to leave tomorrow."

"I need to ask her some questions that could be upsetting. Is she medicated?"

"I'm right here," Lily said. "No, I am not on medication."

"We talked to her physician, and except for a local when we patched up the head wound, she hasn't needed anything for the pain."

"But what about—"

"I told you. I'm in recovery," Lily said. "They know about that little PTSD episode after the first murder. I'm fine now."

"She's a trouper, Detective. Anybody else who'd been through what this young woman has endured would not be so calm." The doctor turned to Lily. "I'll be back to see you in the morning, and if all goes well through the night, we'll discharge you before noon."

After the doctor left, Paxton finally released Lily's hand, so he could call Nigel with an update. "Let's find that room she was kept in—we'll get a sketch of her abductor tomorrow."

Then he turned off his phone, put it away, and said, "I am so glad you're okay."

She smiled but said she was fine, he could go.

"It's my day off," he told her. Not that he'd taken a day off since this case began, but he didn't want her to fret about anything. She'd been through enough.

"Ric." Nobody ever called him that. His family called him Derrick, had never used a shortened version. They liked their formality, his folks, but he liked how Lily said his name. "I'm gonna be okay. You can leave."

"Not yet. I want to hear about why you think your dad had you abducted."

"Not just that. I think he had Roseann and Kennedy killed. It's payback. What else could it be? Who else knew what my childhood bedroom looked like?"

"Friends?"

"Yeah, I don't have any of those. I didn't stay in touch with people after college, and I didn't get close to anybody while I was training for my PI license."

"Why would your father kill your client's wife?"

"I know it seems over the top, but you have his back story. He had my mother killed. So, that's his MO. He hires hit men. And Bingo's in jail. He's done time before. That old man is pulling the strings. I just know it. If you can put Papa and Bingo in the same prison, even for a short time, there's your connection."

Paxton thought Lily's story was full of holes, but he wasn't going to tell her that. She'd been viciously attacked and held in a cell for days. She wanted to make sense of her world again, and that meant stitching up this crime so it made sense. "I'll check out the prison connection. You get some rest."

"Can you do it now? I mean, it's not even dark out yet."

"I don't want to leave you."

She gave his hand one last squeeze. "You have work to do. We can hold hands after I get out of here if you want," she said. She smiled at him and shook her head. "Ow," she said, putting a hand to her bandages.

"You're going to have some hairstyle issues to consider."

She laughed.

He noted her lack of fear. That decided him. "You're right. I should be out there, finding Twitch Eye, photographing the crime scene, checking out your theory regarding your father."

"It feels good having you here," she said. "But it will feel better knowing you're out there when I can't be."

****

The next afternoon Paxton got a text from Lily asking him to bring her some clothes. Then another wanting to know what he'd found out about her dad and Bingo. Then a final one telling him she was being discharged and could he please pick her up.

Her suite at the casino was now a crime scene, but he didn't want to get into that through a text. He made a quick stop at Macy's, snagged a sales clerk, asked her to choose a complete set of "everything" in a size six. Shoes included. She asked if he wanted shorts and a tank top and sandals or jeans and a T-shirt, and he said jeans would be fine. She asked for a bra size and he said "medium" which made her smirk. She got to work, skipping through the departments while he waited at the cash register.

****

"We found where they were keeping you." He handed over the Macy's bag.

"Grim, am I right?" She went off to the bathroom to change.

Seeing that makeshift jail cell, which had once held

the safe and some of the most valuable antiques in the store, made him angry. The original owner had died long ago, and they were tracking down the current owner. "They" were the cops assigned to Lily's case. It wasn't homicide, so it wasn't his case.

But he'd gone anyway, to see that place, that part of town she'd been trapped in. He felt humbled and grateful she was alive. How she'd coped so well confounded him. Somebody had done a head trip on her, and she didn't know the half of it, but she was stronger than he'd known. She'd pull through.

She was dressed and discharged in record time. On the way down to the station, where she'd work with a sketch artist, he told her parts of what he'd discovered since he'd left her the day before.

"I checked out Bingo's record. He wasn't in with your father." Paxton knew incarcerated criminals ruled kingdoms outside their prison walls, but Van Slyke— that had been Lily's last name before she changed it— was not a known member of any organized crime inside. Certainly, he was no leader. He was a bad guy who'd gone down for murder. The cases had an eerie symmetry, but Bingo and Van Slyke had not been aware of each other's existence.

At the station, she described Twitch Eye as having a very apparent tic in the left eye only, and as "looking squirrely around here." She framed the space between her nose and upper lip with her hands.

"Define 'squirrely,' " the sketch artist said.

"He had a tiny overbite on his two front teeth, and the skin looked puffy like those ladies who get Botox. There was a wispy sort of half mustache."

The artist sketched away on his special laptop

program, but Paxton saw him smirk at her depiction. After she'd finished, Paxton brought her into his office while the officers on the case handled the details of getting out the sketches and an APB.

"I just need to fill in some gaps in the report."

"You get it that Jimmy didn't do this."

"Right. But nobody's connecting your kidnapping with the double homicide."

"You're kidding."

"It could be any one of the people you caught on tape defrauding their insurance companies."

"So just a coincidence? Two separate cases?"

She had a stunned look on her face as if she'd never even considered it before. Knowing Lily, she was not considering it now.

"As far as the department's concerned, yes."

"What about you? Do you think they're linked?" She spoke looking out his window. Nothing to see but cars and concrete.

"I'm not sure. So, let's hear the story about your dad. When did you first suspect your father had hired your mother's murder?"

"You have to have a file on that. I mean, the whole story was all over the press."

She must be counting cars because she still wasn't looking at him. He needed her to be more with him than this. He had some unpleasant news to share with her, and he wanted them on the same page moving forward.

"I never heard it from you, from the beginning. Okay if I tape it?"

"Sure. Okay, I first suspected my father killed my mother once my cousin was dead. I had PTSD bad at the time, but I didn't know it. I knew I was jumpy, I could be a real bitch, I had intimacy issues and a drinking problem. Well, who doesn't at that age? So I stumbled along like that for years, and I had a kind of coping thing in college. I learned to shoot. I wasn't planning on shooting him. I just felt safer on campus, and then out in the world, with a gun. With a way to protect myself. And so I had that and my film studies, and I dated, well, not dated, but I hooked up. That's what you do in college right? Nothing serious."

Paxton nodded, but he was only being kind. He'd been in love in college. He'd been so happy with that girl for part of sophomore and then the entire junior year. Five years later, he fell again, had been happily married, too, for a time. He'd been single longer than all those years put together. Maybe that was why he was feeling this pull toward Lily, why he could still feel the blades of her shoulders and the soft swish of her hair against his skin when he put his arm around her, guiding her into his office. He knew he'd catch shit about that later from his co-workers, but he didn't care. That in itself was alarming.

"There was this guy though," Lily continued. "He was always crazy about me. I mean, he hung in there for five years, and really, I gave him no cause. We went to different schools, didn't see each other summers, nothing. But then I got a job in his town after we graduated, and I had this plan. It was a stupid plan, but I was going to find my cousin. It wouldn't be hard; he worked for my dad. I was going to get him in a room, hold a gun on him, and videotape him telling my father that he'd raped me and then he killed my mother because she believed me. And he was evil. I was really grieving my mom at that time. She'd only been dead six months, and it was hard. So, I had to do something. And that was it. That was the entire master plan. Nuts, huh?"

Paxton was recording and taking notes, but when she started to get off track a little bit, he stopped. He still listened, not because he wanted to know every single thing about her or because her voice had suddenly become precious to him, but because you never knew what little thing would turn out to be crucial.

"So this guy—Bob was his name. Yep. Bob was in love with me. And he listened to my plan, and he was going along with it. We were having a thing, a sexual relationship, by this time. I didn't love him. I thought I was flawed that way, where I probably could never really love a man. I didn't know how it felt—to feel the way other people did, joined at the hip, staring into each other's eyes, constantly on the phone if not together. But Bob had that, and I thought, you know, that might be enough. He'd love me, I'd do my best to imitate how he did it, and who knew? Maybe someday the magic would happen to me. And I did like Bob. I had warm feelings toward him."

Paxton saw her notice he was not writing.

"Okay, your question was about when I first suspected my father had hired someone to kill my mother. It was after I killed my cousin. You know about that. Justified homicide. And did you know how my mother died? Supposed car accident? So guess who shows up dead after my cousin was already gone? The mechanic who worked on her car!"

"Quite a coincidence."

"Yeah. I had been trying to track him down

because Bob told me about how he could have tampered with the brakes and nobody would know."

Paxton remembered that. Water in the brake fluid.

Lily took a couple of deep breaths. "I never wanted to think about this stuff again. I left my old life behind when I came to Detroit. But being in that bedroom, my old bedroom, brought everything back. It's all I can think about now. Because I have another score to settle. With my dad, this time. Anyway, you know the next part. It has to be in your file.

"Tell me anyway."

She gritted her teeth, but continued. "So it had to be my dad who killed the mechanic. Or had him killed. To ensure his silence about tampering with my mom's brakes. By this time, my PTSD had got so much worse. I couldn't get it to go underground."

Paxton watched for signs that her PTSD was coming forward again. He didn't really understand how her recovery worked. Most people needed a calm environment, and many of them had trained therapy dogs. She had nobody. Well, she had him. She just didn't know it yet.

"Underground?"

"Yeah, like with my own rape, which is when the first episode happened, I kind of held it underwater. It's not that I blacked it out, but more submerged it. For years. I ran away once, but my mom found me and I went away to college. Took my courses, shot video, and did target practice with my gun. Having those goals and that focus kept me somewhat cool. But after the mechanic died and I realized my own father had killed my mother, I couldn't think straight. Even with therapy and medication, I was messed up. Did I tell you I was staying with Bob's family? And how great they were to me? But it was like I was sealed off from their concern by a thick sheet of plastic. Nothing quite touched me except my symptoms. So I left town. The video was getting a lot of attention, and people were offering me jobs. I didn't take it all in. But one editor of an online newspaper texted, asked if I was going to do any more investigative reporting. I got a new phone number after that, but the idea of investigation stuck in my head. I looked up what all went into becoming a PI, and it was a lot. If you're not a lawyer or a cop, you start from the bottom, right? But that's how I had pulled myself through before, intense study. So I went for it. And I stayed in therapy, and I kept up target practice."

Paxton nodded. Most of the facts were in the file, but not how she felt, how she walked through the world.

"And then you saw the video where I got my dad to confess on tape."

"It was very good work for someone with no training." He'd always thought that. But he had to keep the compliments in check.

"I had the degree in videography."

"I meant the way you drew him out."

"I took a bunch of psych classes in college. I did a shitload of outside reading. So I knew about psychopaths. I figured my dad had to be on that spectrum somewhere. I thought maybe he could be a narcissist too. So my idea was simple: genetics. I'd pretend to be like him. We'd both killed someone. Cold-blooded. I pretended I didn't care about killing my cousin when the truth is I wish it hadn't been necessary. I don't like living with the knowledge that

I've killed someone, even in those circumstances where I had to kill to save an innocent life."

Paxton nodded. He knew all about complicated regrets.

"So I asked my dad—you hear it on the tape—if there was something missing in us, that we could do things like that. He bought it. I was his mini-me."

She paused. He didn't want to lead her. He'd seen that video several times, so he knew what happened next, but he wanted it in her words.

"He let down his guard and said some things— honestly, I've never watched the video, and I've mostly blanked out the exact words I used. But my hidden cameras caught him confessing on tape. I put it up on YouTube the minute he drove away."

Paxton nodded. He really didn't want to have to tell her what he'd discovered online yesterday after he'd left the hospital. It was still shocking to him, and he was still going over what to do about it. He knew he had to tell Lily, but beyond that, he had to figure out a way to protect her.

"You had your own channel, right?" He stopped recording, stopped taking notes. For now, he had everything he needed. He just had to fill in a few blanks for her. And they'd figure out the rest together.

"Sure. In college. I was a videographer. We all posted those clips. It was kind of a thing at the time. Some of that crap was even graded."

"But you never took your videos down."

She had been studying her fingernails. The chipped red polish from yesterday had disappeared, and the natural nails were neatly trimmed. She looked up at him now, alert to something she didn't know coming at her even before she could see it.

"No. Why?"

"I've seen them. A few of them were filmed in your childhood bedroom. Must have been summer vacation."

"My furniture." She made the connection right away.

He nodded.

"I forgot. Damn. How could I have forgotten? So somebody else, not my father, could have set up that room. Found the same furniture on eBay. But why? Who would have a motive except him? I'm the one who landed him in jail."

As she spoke, he saw her turning over the possibilities in her mind.

"How smart a guy do you figure Twitch Eye is?"

"Not very."

"Okay. And Bingo's behind bars. No bail for him."

She stared into her lap, but he felt her mind working, trying to catch up. She didn't have all the facts yet. But then neither did he. He had a little more information than she did, though, and he wasn't sure how she'd react to it.

"Think about it, Ric. Do you really think Jimmy would lock me up because he saw some old video I made in college?"

"I don't think so. There's more."

He clicked on the first link and turned his laptop to face her across the desk so she could see the video her captor had made of her locked in the room that so closely resembled her childhood bedroom.

Her face turned white, and her eyes fluttered after the last frame.

He got up and around his desk and touched his hand to the back of her neck. "Put your head down. Take some deep breaths."

She did as he asked but didn't stay down long. "It's nothing, Ric. I need coffee, okay?"

"Yeah, fine," he said. "But you're wrong. It's not nothing. Someone has a very sick interest in you."

"It's like I said. My dad's behind it."

Paxton didn't believe that, but he didn't argue with her. She'd been through enough. "Let's get out of here."

Chapter 15

Lily

Ric asked me if I wanted something to eat with my coffee, and I nodded. I didn't care about food, but I was too busy detaching from the things on the film he'd just shown me, the depictions that made me seem like a person with a serious substance abuse problem. Was I? Dr. Cam would solve that puzzle.

I realized, standing there in the coffee shop, leaning against Ric's suit jacket, that something else had changed; he wasn't Paxton anymore. He was Ric. I had told him all my secrets. I'd laid my messed-up life bare. The way he responded, with his comforting touch, with the gentle way he accompanied me, with coffee, felt more intimate than any of those times I'd taken off my clothes for boys.

I didn't have a phone or a car. I didn't have a credit card or a driver's license. I should feel deeply anxious about those things, but, because Ric was there, I knew everything would be okay. It was as if he had dismantled another jail cell, a stronger one than where I'd been held for the last few days. I was suddenly free from the place inside that for as long as I could remember had kept me a little bit apart from the rest of the world.

"Thank you," I said, as the barista handed me my

coffee. I smiled at her. I'm not a smiley person, probably closer to the opposite, but it just happened and I went with it.

Ric had gotten our order to go. We went back out into the day, and I appreciated the sun and the air and the sky. All that monkey-mind meditation in the makeshift jail cell had done me more good than I'd thought. At the time, it seemed the only way not to go insane. But it had done more. Since waking up in the hospital yesterday, I felt a kind of peace I'd never known. Even when I viewed that first video in Ric's office: me in captivity in a room set like a stage of my old bedroom. I hadn't come off too bad. It was a pretty boring video, edited down to two minutes of me screaming for someone to let me out. Yeah, I might have been screaming, but the look on my face was not terror or panic. It was rage. I stopped screaming when I figured out nobody was coming and I might as well save my breath. The video showed me going over to the bed and stretching out on it, my eyes seeming to stare right into the camera. That's when the video stopped. Watching someone meditate wouldn't get any clicks.

"That stupid tiled ceiling," I told Ric. "I looked for a camera in there but didn't find it. It must have been microscopic."

Ric nodded, coming over to my side of the car and opening the door. I scooted in.

"Want your scone?" Ric said, handing me the brown paper bag.

I nodded, opened the bag, finished the pastry in two bites.

"Can we go to my place now?" The sip of coffee I swallowed worked its magic. I was starting to build a mental to-do list.

He was silent a beat. Two. "The suite's a crime scene, so we can't go there. I'm taking you to my place."

"Wait! What? Why is my place a crime scene?"

"Initially I just went in because we, me and Melanie, were worried about you. I did a pretty thorough sweep, which is how I found the cameras with more videotape."

Ric kept his eyes on the road, his hands on the wheel. I could tell he was checking to see if anyone was following us.

"Is there video of me naked? Like getting dressed or in the bath?"

"No. We haven't found anything like that. The crime scene techs found three surveillance cameras, and they each had particular angles. The sofa, the bathroom sink, the bedside table. They've viewed the footage. There are a few more uploads on YouTube. Whoever did this used your old channel."

I thought about what the released video might show: me drinking wine and taking meds, probably edited to look continuous but truly happening over a period of time. That's how I'd cut it, to make me look like a drunk and a pill addict. Because I was a videographer myself, I couldn't help worrying that the guy who'd taped me may have come and gone while I was in my cell. He may have more cameras than the police had found, more footage than he'd put on my video channel. Worse footage. I needed to get busy and delete that old channel. Even thinking this, I knew it was probably all over other people's video feeds and would never really go away, no matter what I did. I needed to stop worrying and focus.

"If they found the recording devices, why is my place still a crime scene?"

"Our lab thinks the same person who did the tape of you in the cell did the others, too. And that's probably the person who kidnapped you. What if that kidnapper comes for you again? I need to make sure you're safe."

"I just want to look at everything the crime lab has of me on tape. And any other videos that were released on my channel. So please give me your phone. Now."

"At my place."

I got a really bad feeling when we stopped at the light, and Ric still didn't hand over his phone. What else was out there? If I Googled my name, what was I going to see? The light turned green. We were rolling again, and my thoughts roared past the speed limit, turning weird corners.

"This isn't about your partner? The one with PTSD who shot himself?"

"What? I'm not getting the connection," Ric said.

"Are you sure you're not in this with me because you feel guilty about him?" I knew all about Trevor. I'd done an investigation of my own on Ric. Knew about his ex-wife, how she'd left Detroit for LA in the hopes of landing a cooking show. That hadn't happened, but she was an assistant to an assistant at a local news channel so she was at least somewhere with her dreams. I wondered if she ever regretted the way she just up and left him.

Then there was all that training Ric had taken in PTSD. I knew cops didn't usually admit to having the disorder, but Ric was now trained to spot mental disruption in a fellow officer. Or a friend. "Are you atoning for your sins here?"

"No. I don't even know what that means."

"Well, I'm trying to figure out why you're being so super nice to me."

"I care about you, Lily. I want to protect you. Find out who did this to you."

I cared about Ric too, but I didn't have practice in sayings those kinds of things. "There's no murder here. So it's not your case."

"Right, it's a separate investigation, but I'm keeping an eye on things. Because, as I mentioned, I care about you."

I was silent. He was nice. Probably too nice for me, but we had a certain rapport. I liked talking about the case with him. I still thought of the double homicide and the kidnapping as all part of one big conspiracy plot.

"The guy behind everything is Papa," I said. "He wanted my case to fail in a spectacular fashion. He wanted me to feel guilty and ashamed for getting two good people killed. He wanted my client to be convicted, which would do me no good in my chosen profession. He wanted me spooked and feeling like I was on hidden camera. He wanted to flare my panic. He wanted to make me pay. And he wanted to do it in such a way that he could never be blamed."

Ric didn't respond to that. Instead he said, "My building is high security. You'll be safe there."

"Crap," I said.

"What?" Ric asked. "There's a great view. A nice guest suite."

"No, not that. I'm sure your place is swank." In

truth, I was having doubts about staying at Ric's. I like living alone. But I tried to push aside my misgivings and focus on what came next. "All my video equipment was in the SUV. All my credit cards and my phone were with me too. I need a car. I need clothes."

"At least you've got your Kimber."

"Yes. Thank you." Ric had pulled strings to get my favorite firearm out of evidence and back to me. I hadn't shot a target in days, and my trigger finger itched.

"I took care of the credit cards when we found your car. And your phone was found ruined in a Dumpster close to where you were held. The weapon you were carrying is gone, but it shouldn't take long, maybe a day, for the crime-scene people to go over your place."

My place. Somehow, knowing Papa's goons had been there, who knows how many times, or when, made me cringe on the inside. Outside, I kept myself together as we turned north on Jefferson. Uptown. Then my mind caught up with something he'd said.

"How did you know my credit card numbers?"

"I'm a police detective."

"You've been in my suite." I didn't feel invaded or anything. At least not by Ric. "It doesn't even seem like my suite anymore. I'm glad you were there, that the police are taking this seriously. Someone out there is stalking me the way Bingo stalked Roseann." I shuddered, aware that my earlier peace of mind had fled. "No. This is worse. Twitch Eye was hired, like Bingo was hired." I wasn't going to push the theory of my father as evil mastermind on Ric. He wasn't convinced, I could tell.

"The department likes one of the Heyl brothers for

the murders."

"It doesn't make sense that Jimmy or Dan would kidnap me."

"The department doesn't see the cases as connected."

"What about you?"

"I just want to keep you safe and find evidence. Find Twitch Eye."

"For sure, there's a piece or two missing. I still feel like Jimmy was being set up by someone for reasons unknown. Or I'm slotting my father into the 'unknown,' and I do this because I have a perfect reason: I put him in prison for life, Ric."

"I'm not saying you're wrong. And I agree this thing is looking a little less cut and dried than I thought at first. I don't see Jimmy kidnapping you and setting up a videotape and all of that. He's been in our line of vision every minute. If he had some kind of bozo crime syndicate, we'd know. And Dan, well, the best he can do is run a bar. And an illegal marijuana business. Let's see if we can get something out of Twitch Eye when we bring him in."

Ric might not think my client had me abducted, but it sounded like Detroit PD was going to pursue double homicide charges anyway. Ric said there'd been enough of a mess with Dan's financials to put together a tenuous case against him, and maybe they'd say it was a crime of passion, or maybe they'd say he set up the hits for Jimmy.

"I need to get a phone." And a new purse. Among other things. "I have to contact my client." If the cops tried to pin the murders on Dan, he'd be livid. I thought about that for a second. "I need to buy a car, too. Like, today."

Ric nodded. "We'll get to all that," he said as he pulled up at an elegant high-rise that faced the Detroit River. There was a guy to park the car in an underground garage, a muscular young doorman who held open a glass door, and a guy behind a marble desk who buzzed us in. They all looked like they spent a lot of time at the gym. I wondered if the glass doors in front were bulletproof.

Ric introduced me to Walter, the reception guy. "Lily is going to be staying with me for a while. She'll need a key." I mulled this statement over and did a mental check on how I felt about it while the guy took a picture of me for his computer. He clicked away at for a few seconds, adding me into the system. I added "staying with Ric" to my reality, and it sat a little shaky. I'd lived alone for a long time, and I liked it. Then the concierge handed me a key. "Welcome to the building, Ms. White."

The elevator was silent and swift. So was my mental process. Ric and I had been on a few dates. We'd been boating and out to dinner, and we'd chased a criminal. I'd met his family. We'd held hands at the hospital. Where were we heading besides up this elevator?

"What is this? An apartment? A condo?" I tried to be casual.

Ric shrugged. "I rent," he said.

"Did your wife live here with you?"

"No. I moved in here when we split up."

That was a relief. I didn't need any of his ghosts around. I had enough of my own. Maybe that was selfish of me. He listened to all my sad stories. Should I offer to hear about his? I knew the facts, but not how he felt about them. "Did it hurt for a long time? When she left?"

"I got over it eventually," he said as the elevator doors opened to a foyer. There were four doors; Ric swiped his key card through the one to the right of the elevator. Okay, guess that discussion was over. For now. Ric put his hand on my waist and urged me into another foyer, with wood floors instead of white carpet. And windows across a large open living and dining space. Outside the sparkling clean windows, the skyline soared, and the river glittered in the hot sun.

Ric was already heading to the left where a curved staircase with floating steps led, I guessed, to the bedrooms. I followed him because I knew my gun was somewhere in his big leather cop bag where he kept his evidence kit and his handcuffs. And also, I wanted to see that video Ric had shown me earlier and any other videos he hadn't. I asked him again for his phone.

He walked across the guest room, unzipped his bag, and set my newly freed Kimber on a low dresser. The room was decorated in beige, black, and brown neutrals. Even the art on the walls, abstract pen and ink sketches, were black and white, in floating frames. The many shades of beige and brown were more beautiful and numerous than I'd ever imagined; the effect was soothing. I noted the queen-sized bed, the desk. I walked farther into the room and picked up my Kimber. I can't explain the way it made me feel complete, having it in my grip. "Do I have a license to carry?"

Ric pulled two smallish laminated cards out of his wallet and handed them to me, gesturing toward a walk-in closet that led to a bathroom. Too bad I didn't have any clothes to hang in the closet or a laptop for the desk. But I had my Kimber and firearm permit plus a copy of my PI license. It was a start.

"Thank you," I said.

"My sister picked up a toothbrush and some other stuff. She said she'd leave it in the bathroom."

I paused a beat. Did that mean Ric's entire family had keys to this place? That any one of them could walk in on me any time they pleased? I was only slightly getting used to the fact that I'd be staying with him, at least for a day or two. But I couldn't handle sisters with keys coming in and catching me unaware. He must have read my mind. That or the horrified expression on my face.

"I had Walter let her in. Nobody except top security has keys but you and me."

Ric's phone rang. He picked up. "Yeah," he said. "Okay. Give me thirty." He clicked off his phone and said, "They've got somebody who fits the description of Twitch Eye."

"That was fast."

"Lineup in an hour. Are you ready?"

"No. I want to use your phone to view those videos from my rooms at the Iroquois. And brush my teeth."

Ric opened the top drawer in the dresser. Inside were some clothes and a red leather purse. Ric's sister again?

"Thank you. And thank your sister for me."

"You'll probably be able to get your stuff from the suite tomorrow, but just in case, I wanted you to be comfortable." He had his phone out and was clicking around. The video. Ric handed me his phone. Just as I'd thought, in frame after frame, I reached for a bottle or a glass, always red wine, always followed by a great show of dexterity in putting a pill on my tongue with one hand while taking a drink with the other.

My most closely guarded secret, one I didn't even let myself think about, one Dr. Cam didn't know about, was now on public display. I liked to combine benzos and Cabernet. Worked better that way. Worked better, looked worse. After a series of these close-ups, there were more on a slightly different theme. Me, reaching into my purse for my pills. Me, at the bathroom sink, next to my prescription bottle. Me, in the bedroom, taking a bottle of pills from my bedside table and struggling to open the childproof cap. Sometimes I shook out one pill. More often it was two. Or three. At least I wasn't naked in any of them, but my face was clear for anyone interested in the weird fringe of life online.

An uninformed viewer might think that the other video in the fake bedroom was some kind of hardcore rehab. Which was pretty accurate. I clicked off the video and handed Ric his phone. Taking long, measured breaths, I lifted the purse out of the drawer. Inside, there was a matching wallet. Both the purse and the wallet were brand new. I slipped my permits and my key card into the wallet and my Kimber into the purse.

"Okay?" I asked Ric. I hadn't forgotten the lineup we were heading to next. I couldn't conceal a weapon in a cop shop. But I needed the Kimber with me.

"You can lock it in my trunk," he said.

"Okay. Then I'm ready."

As soon as I identified Twitch Eye, I'd get my gun from Ric's car. I'd Uber over to the bank, then to the closest SUV dealer and pick up whatever was on the lot. I had shopping to do. Maybe if I had some things around me that were mine, sharing living space wouldn't bother me so much.

****

The room where the lineup was taking place already had another person in the room when Ric, his partner, and I came in. A woman with some tech equipment. Instead of glass like you see in the movies, she turned on a giant flat-screen television. There were lines for height and shoe imprints on the floor where the guys were supposed to stand. She checked off something, then the screen went blank.

She had a headset and listened to someone saying something. After a few minutes, she flipped the screen again. And there, amidst a group of grungy men, was Twitch Eye, standing in front of me. I knew in that moment I'd never eat a slider again. For me, the smell of them would forever be associated with Twitch Eye's sweaty armpit.

"That's him," I said without hesitation. "Number three," I clarified. Above each of the guys, there was a number on the wall. There were lines, too, from the number to the floor, to mark the lanes. Nobody asked me to look again or if I was certain I had the right man. The television clicked off, the tech left the room, Nigel stood. Ric put this arm around me and hugged me tight to his chest. "You did terrific, baby."

I called a car service from that room, and Ric walked me down to the main floor and out to his car, where he popped the trunk so I could retrieve my Kimber. He waited with me for my driver to arrive. When a sleek steel-colored car pulled up, Ric looked into my eyes and said, "Stay safe."

I nodded.

"I'm having a marked unit follow you today. Just a precaution. But you'll know it's one of us."

"Thanks," I said. As I settled into the back seat of the car, I remembered Ric calling me baby in front of his partner. I liked the way it sounded, and I knew I shouldn't. I'm nobody's baby. That's what I would have said a week ago. Today was different.

Chapter 16

Paxton

Paxton sat, both feet flat on the floor. He was halfway through an uncomfortable meeting with his father. The chief sat behind his imposing desk while Paxton was relegated to a hard-backed chair that wobbled if he moved. His dad used that chair on purpose, he'd often said, to keep people on their toes. The chief had already told Paxton he had no business nosing around the investigation into Lily's kidnapping, and that the task force Paxton headed needed to issue an arrest warrant for Dan Heyl. Now he was grilling Paxton on his new living arrangements, details provided, no doubt, by Paxton's sister.

"It's not that she's white, although that doesn't help. It's that she's working for a murder suspect. She's in the case up to her neck. It's a huge conflict of interest."

"Chief, no disrespect, but you didn't think it was a conflict of interest to use her video to catch the hit man. Listen, my personal life is just that, personal. As to the warrant, we've got a meeting in ten minutes, and I will convey your ultimatum to the task force." Then he got up and without waiting to be dismissed, left the room.

The group gathered one floor down in the largest meeting room. Paxton got right down to brass tacks.

"Despite lack of hard evidence, we're going to use Dan Heyl's banking irregularities to secure an arrest warrant."

"For Dan Heyl?" Nigel asked.

"Yes."

"Maybe Jimmy Heyl will then confess out of brotherly love," one of the uniforms said.

Everybody laughed.

"We know Dan Heyl's weed business results in irregular banking, a hundred or two at a time, in and out almost daily. This loosely fits with what was deposited into Bingo's account. Then there's the fact that they both use Diablo's storefront for money transfers." Paxton looked at his men. Most of them were obviously relieved to make an arrest. Any arrest.

"What about Dan Heyl's weed trade? That's strictly a cash operation," Nigel pointed out.

"We're ignoring that." Again, Paxton checked out the uniforms who had been brought in to work the case with him and Nigel. Nobody blinked.

One smart ass said, "Let him try to use that as his defense." Again, more relieved laughter. Federal law prohibited marijuana sales. The states with legalization laws were forced to work on a cash basis.

"So, while there's no hard evidence linking Dan and Bingo, there's enough there to raise the level of probability." Paxton ended the meeting.

He asked Nigel to handle the warrant. Everybody was happy the investigation was over, the bad guy all but booked. But Paxton had a hard feeling in his gut that Dan Heyl was a scapegoat. A sacrificial lamb. And nobody, not even Nigel, cared except Paxton. Paxton still believed Jimmy might have hired a hit on his wife and her boyfriend, but it was all Dan could do to get his liquor order straight. The guy used too much of his product to put together a double homicide, scant hours and distance apart. Could he get lucky and hire someone smarter than he was? Sure, but that someone was not Bingo Banks.

Paxton couldn't dismiss the idea that the Heyl brothers were innocent of murder. He wasn't sure when this rock had settled in his stomach, but now he felt he should have looked harder at Victory Motors. He had discounted Lily's conspiracy theory at the time. And even now...Lily's father as mastermind of the conspiracy seemed too far a stretch, even for a man in love. He didn't like admitting, even to himself, that he was falling for Lily, but in fact he was on a fast train running downhill. He wondered. Did she feel the same?

After a long day, Paxton entered his apartment to the smell of something burning. Lily, he knew, was home. Funny how he thought that, as if her being here was home. He headed into the kitchen, his mostly unused kitchen, if you didn't count the coffee machine. Lily stood over the stove, a spatula in her hand, a large kitchen towel tucked around the waist of brand new jean shorts. She was scraping at burned eggs.

"Breakfast for dinner," she said, smiling at him. "After I went to the DMV and the car dealership and did a little more personal shopping and made a few phone calls on my new phone." She pulled it out of the back pocket of her jean shorts and held it out like a display so he could see the rose gold color. "I went to the fancy organic grocery store on Mack and bought out the place."

Toast popped, and bacon sizzled. She'd found

every appliance his mother and sisters had bought him from the griddle to the toaster to the pan of eggs that was probably ruined.

She'd turned off the cooktop burner but left the pan of blackened eggs on the stove. She turned on the exhaust fan. It was loud. He'd never used it.

"Never mind," she said, nodding at the eggs. "We have toast and bacon, and I bought tomatoes! We'll have BLTs."

Paxton wanted to wrap his arms around her as she flipped the bacon on the griddle with a fork. He ached to kiss the side of her face where her hair got curly from the heat in the kitchen. He felt a bit stunned by the newly domestic Lily. By her being here, in his place. Snap out of it, he told himself. He loved her. He did. It was just strange, that's all.

"Will you open a bottle of wine?" Lily asked. Her smile was wide. She didn't seem to have a care in the world.

He opened the wine she pushed toward him, then reached around and spread paper towels on the countertop to soak up the bacon grease. Lily got the bacon off before it burned. It smelled so good. She smelled good. Somewhere in her shopping today, she must have bought a new bottle of that perfume she always wore. He didn't know the name of it, but he knew the scent. Wildflowers.

"How'd it go? What did you find out?" She sliced tomatoes and tore lettuce as he unplugged the griddle.

"Twitch Eye is Douglas Danz. He's local. He fingered his accomplice, the one you didn't see, as Franklin Roosevelt Jones, known locally as Ank."

She waited, the half-made sandwiches forgotten.

He wasn't sure how to tell her that Danz and Jones had shed no light. Or none that he could share. Although the official line was that the homicides were not connected to the kidnapping, there was a glaring coincidence. Both hit man and kidnapper had been paid from Diablo's corner store that sold lottery tickets and beer, cashed paychecks, and advanced funds "anywhere in the world" via a barely legal backroom setup. The place had no surveillance cameras, which very effectively cut off the trail of small change that went into petty criminals' accounts. "So we're no further along than we were before."

"What about the IP address for the stupid videos?"

"The original is gone. So many people shared it that whoever uploaded it first was easily able to erase themselves."

"What about my father?"

Paxton took her hand, which still held the knife she'd cut the tomatoes with. He felt her fist relax under his touch. She set down the knife. "There's one strange thing about the guys who took you. Danz is white, but Jones is black."

"Why's that weird?"

They were going somewhere he hadn't expected quite this soon. He hadn't meant to share quite so much. He delayed replying by snagging two glasses from a cabinet and pouring the wine.

"How about some wine? I'll explain everything over dinner."

She said, "Be right back," and ran out of the room.

Not sure what to do, he assembled the sandwiches. She came back with a candle and a book of matches. She turned off the fan over the stove and whipped the towel from her waist, throwing it on the countertop. She looked so hot in those jean shorts. He pulled his head out of the soft edge of skin showing between her shorts and top and dragged himself back into the room.

The smoke had dissipated, but the smell of burnt eggs lingered. She lit the candle and set it on the table. "This will get rid of the burnt-egg smell." She took a bite of her sandwich and a sip of her wine. "Okay. What's weird about Jones and Danz working together?"

"It's unusual for a black brother to work with a white nationalist."

"Ugh. White nationalists. That's like those guys, Boots and Skinny, at Dan Heyl's bar. I told you about them. What they said about you...and me. D'ya think there's a connection?"

Paxton chewed his sandwich, choosing his words carefully. There was so much he couldn't say. Not yet. Maybe not ever. "I'm not sure. It might not feel that way to us, but the truth is Detroit is one of the most racially divided cities in the nation."

"You wouldn't think so," she said. "Not in this century."

Her attitude was that of a normal naïve white person, but she lived in a casino. Casinos in Detroit, particularly the one she lived above, were mostly well integrated, what with native American, Asian, Hispanic, black, and white all agreeing on one thing: they liked throwing their money away. Although, Windsor across the river was known as the "white" casino, and the new "D" in midtown was the "black" one.

They still hadn't really touched on this basic thing between them. "We've been on a couple of dates," Paxton said. "That makes us an interracial couple in a city that isn't all that happy to accommodate us." He needed to veer away from discussion of Franklin Roosevelt Jones.

"You're saying if our relationship continues, and things get more serious, it won't always be easy for us," she said.

"Yes. And now that you live here, some will assume we've gone to that next level already."

"It's not a big deal. We should be able to hang out if we want to, and I don't think anybody is going to stop us." She huffed out a breath. "I talked to Melanie today. She said I can stay with her while I look for a place in the West Village. I told you I wanted to move there. Right?"

She said it like it was no big deal. But he wondered how long their "friendship" would last if she thought her kidnapping was because she'd been seen around town with a black man. He wasn't sure that's what her kidnapping had been about. He'd never dated a white woman, didn't want the hassle. Now, he was in it. There was no way out. He didn't want out. Not that he was afraid of a little bit of trouble. Hell, if she could be so breezy about it, then he could handle it, too. Also, they had other problems.

"Work is crazy right now. We've got Bingo, Danz, and Jones. Looks like the department is going to settle for that." He left out the imminent arrest of her client's brother. Until it happened, he couldn't say a word. Not to her, not to anyone.

"What...so...the person behind all of this just gets off?"

He topped off her glass of wine.

"I know. It goes against everything I believe in, but

that's the way it works sometimes."

She ignored her wine. "Well, then fine. Let's do this together, me and you."

He studied her. She had been through so much. But she was a fighter.

"Don't you have vacation time coming up?"

He did. He never took vacations. Not since—well, not since his divorce.

"Okay, you know I kept thinking my father had to be behind this, just because, unlike my client, who by the way is still paying me to find the guy who hired Bingo, he has a motive. Revenge. So I have to see my father. I'm going to visit him. Tomorrow. You can come with me. After all, I met your family. Now you can meet mine."

Not only had Lily renewed her driver's license, bought a phone and a car, not only had she gone grocery shopping, but she'd arranged a visit to her father at the correctional facility outside Ann Arbor where he was serving a long sentence. And she was going with or without Paxton. He preferred with. He called the night supervisor at headquarters and arranged a few days of vacation. He had to somehow talk Lily into staying with him for a while. Danz and Jones were on record as hired hands. The person who kidnapped Lily was still at large. He wanted to find that person before Lily moved anywhere.

They washed the dishes together because there weren't enough to fill the dishwasher. He dried because he knew what went where. He opened a discreet chute at the side of the sink and threw away the burned pan, eggs and all.

"I'm going to shower." He started to leave the

room, then stopped and turned toward her. "Please don't go to Melanie's. Stay with me. Let's find your kidnapper together."

"You said the department thinks Danz and Jones are good enough."

This is where he had to keep his damn mouth shut, or change the subject. "I'm on vacation. Like you said, we team up to get these cases solved."

"You are awesome," she said. And there came that smile again. She was a lovely woman, but that smile took her face to a whole other level of beautiful.

Chapter 17

Lily

Last night, Ric and I had dinner like a real couple. This morning, the soft spray of water from the shower made me feel not just clean, but new. Something sweet and thrilling swirled on my skin, sending joyful messages to my head and heart. Nothing in my life thus far compared. My only other real relationship had been with Bob, and I hadn't felt anything like this; the feelings had mostly been on his side.

Was it just that I was free after being held hostage? Or was it more? I stepped out of the shower and carefully combed my hair, sweeping a deep part from right to left to hide the gash in my skull. I turned to the walk-in closet and the clothes I'd bought for security, so I'd have things of my own hanging here. Ric said my suite would be cleared in a day or two, but after watching the video, I didn't think I'd ever live there again. I didn't think I'd wear my other clothes. What if my stalker had handled my things? That's what the police were finding out, as well as looking for DNA from the intruder who had planted not just one but several microscopic cameras in my home.

I knew there had to be more tape somewhere. As I zipped up a pair of sober dark-wash jeans, I dreaded finding out that I'd aimlessly wandered into the camera view while changing clothes. I pulled on a tank top and then layered a tissue-thin tunic over it, thinking the cameras could have caught me half-dressed, rushing to find my ringing phone or searching the bedside table for hand lotion. There were more questions than answers, but it seemed pretty obvious to me, just by tracking the clothes I'd worn on video, that the cameras had been placed in my suite a few days after the shootings. Three weeks. I didn't yet know if the feed was on a timer so it only captured me for a few hours a day or if the cameras had delivered a live continuous loop on a remote computer.

I slid the ends of my hair between the tongs of a flat iron, trying not to think about how much I wanted a pill. The hospital doctor had asked if I wanted a prescription refill, and I'd said no. I wanted to get back to feeling everything life threw at me. Some parts, like when I thought of the fact that I was living here with Ric, were amazing. But I didn't like knowing there could be more video of me out there, and I dreaded seeing my father. But more than relief, I wanted and needed the edge that medication would dull. As long as I could walk that edge and not slip over into panic, I'd be fine no matter what happened next.

I'd slept in the guest room last night after Ric and I watched the news together. Ric had seemed relieved there was no new reporting on the double homicide his department was trying to pin on my client. I knew something was going on there—why else had he suddenly decided to take a vacation? Were they dropping the case? Or had they decided to arrest someone?

I wound the cord around the flat iron and tucked it

in the cabinet under the sink, pulling out some new makeup I'd picked up yesterday and put on a little blush and mascara. Were jeans appropriate for a prison visit? I gave myself one final look in the mirror. Shaky inside, totally together outside. Shockingly, I'd slept seven hours last night, and my eyes were clear. Apparently, I'd worn myself out yesterday shopping, cooking, and identifying the man who had abducted me.

Now, though, I was uneasy. I didn't want to face Papa. I didn't want to know that monster. The compelling scent of fresh coffee lured me down the stairs. Nerves or not, I needed a cup. I'd been in such full speed mode yesterday; that had always been one of my coping mechanisms. Pile on the work, the errands, the stuff to do, and go at it with single-minded focus. I'd tried on each item of clothing. Everything fit, even the suede ballerina flats I carried down the stairs. I left them at the door and went into the kitchen.

I saw Ric and smiled. He was smiling too and holding a coffee cup toward me. I was more comfortable with Ric in that moment than if we'd gone ahead and slept together. I knew he wanted to. I wanted to, too. But for once in my life, I decided to act smart where men were concerned and take it slow. That wouldn't be easy living together. I needed a place of my own. Just not the Iroquois suite. Tomorrow, I'd call Melanie to see if she knew of any listings in the West Village.

I took the coffee Ric offered. "Thanks," I said. "So, who did they arrest?"

He'd switched off his laptop, which had been playing the local news, when I walked in.

"Sorry," he said. "Dan Heyl."

I sighed into my coffee. "Do you really think he did it?"

Ric shrugged. "Wasn't my call."

In the weeks since the double homicide I'd witnessed, there had been close to a dozen more murders, about average in a city that saw roughly three hundred homicides a year. The police were moving on, making a high-profile arrest that would get reported, and help the city simmer down, make folks feel like the PD had things under control.

"At least *you* are considering that my kidnapping is related to the homicides and that just maybe we can find the truly guilty party behind all of this." I didn't say that the guilty party was already behind bars, but there was no doubt in my mind.

"Sleep okay?" Ric asked.

"Smooth change of subject," I said.

"Let's go," he said, after I finished my coffee and declined toast.

We went down to the parking garage so I could show Ric my new car. I'd texted him a photo yesterday, but I wanted him to see it anyway.

"That's what I thought. Just like the last one."

"Yep. Same color, but it's a newer model." I had loved my SUV and decided almost immediately that low-life criminals were not going to scare me away from replicating it. "You want to drive?"

Ric smiled. "Sure."

We drove in silence until we were well out of the city. My eyes rested on Ric's capable hands steering the wheel. I've always loved driving. Being on the road. Heading for somewhere. Even this drive to see my despised father in prison didn't completely cloud my mood. If the thought of Papa brought a slight shiver of fear, I switched my thoughts from him to Ric. We would solve these seemingly unsolvable crimes. We would defy the odds together.

Such strange facts that didn't seem to fit. What, if anything, did Papa have to do with Jimmy and Roseann Heyl? Thomas Kennedy? Had he somehow hired Jimmy to hire me? Just to mess with me? He must have a lot of time on his hands in prison, because he had never gone to such trouble to disrupt my life before. Well, that wasn't exactly true. He had caused my mother's death. The ultimate disruption.

I looked out the window at the passing scenery to distract myself. We were on a freeway heading west toward Ann Arbor. Like much of Michigan's highways, this one seemed to be the only man-made thing for miles around. The scenery was natural, trees and scrub, leafing out with summer exuberance.

"You okay?" Ric asked.

He wasn't exactly hovering, but he was being very sweet. He'd taken vacation from his own job to help me figure out who had been behind my kidnapping. The Detroit PD was satisfied that the actual people who had done the kidnapping were behind bars. They thought those bozos put together the creepy bedroom scenario and the stupid secret videos of me.

"I'll be better when this is over."

"The visit or the case?"

My mind was mostly just on the visit. I dreaded seeing Papa. But Ric didn't need to hear that. He'd heard enough of me moaning. I wanted to put this behind me; I wanted this drive on a sunny summer day to never end. The bit in the middle, the part where I had to look at the man who had caused me so much misery, that was what was happening now, as the fence and walls of the correctional facility, my father's fancy prison, came into view.

The prison was more of a country club or maybe like one of those rehabilitation centers for ailing rich people. My father was ailing, all right. He was a raging narcissist born without an ounce of empathy. I clenched my damp palms, digging my nails into the flesh, as Ric parked the car. As we walked toward the visitor's entrance, he put his arm around me and gave me a quick one-armed hug. At the gate, we showed ID and were checked off a list. I didn't know how, but somehow Ric had got himself on that list. His presence here made these moments so much softer. We walked through a metal detector just like the ones at the airport. Someone searched my new purse. My Kimber was in a new lockbox in the car.

A guard led us down a hallway. He opened the door to a carpeted room, painted a soothing muted blue, furnished with a sofa and armchair in a complementary shade of navy. Ric and I sat on the sofa together. My knee-jerk reaction to a knock on the door was to grab Ric's hand and hold on tight. The same guard who'd led us to this room opened the door.

Papa shuffled in with a male attendant. His hair had gone white, he'd grown a messy beard, and his shoulders stooped. Then he raised his head, and there was an unmistakable twinkle in his eye. He straightened his shoulders and practically sang out his words.

"Karen!" he said. "You're here." He sounded pleased. Truly happy. I was stunned. Karen was my mother's name. His dead wife's name.

"Papa, stop it." I looked at Ric. "Karen was my mother."

Papa looked confused. He seemed to notice Ric for the first time. He took in our clasped hands.

"Lily?"

The room was large enough, the two prison employees could give us a semblance of privacy by huddling over phones at a small table by the door. I looked with curiosity but no fear at Papa. Gave an involuntary shiver. Hoped he didn't notice.

He laughed. Delighted somehow. "To what do I owe the pleasure?" His voice was devoid of irony.

"I think you know," I said.

"But I don't." He looked past me, his eyes bouncing off walls until he spied his keeper. "Bud, where's my wife? You said she'd be here soon."

The guard who had escorted my father into the room came over and grasped Papa's shoulder, giving it a reassuring squeeze.

"He gets confused sometimes," said Bud, shrugging.

I was sure my father was acting out some elaborate ruse. "What did you do with my furniture when the house was sold?"

Papa smiled. Shrugged. "The details escape me," he said.

"I bet," I said. I suddenly felt like this had been a dead end. He wasn't going to reveal anything. He was going to pretend to have dementia. I never said the old man wasn't smart. Still, I had to try to be smarter. "Does the name Bingo ring any bells? What about Roosevelt Jones?"

I thought I saw a nerve tick in his left eye. Just a

flicker, but it had been there. "No, why should I? Lily, where is your mother? Is this black man your husband?"

I didn't want to introduce Ric to my father.

"Detective Derrick Paxton," Ric said, "Detroit Police."

"That's improper. He's black," Papa said. "Karen must be livid."

I'd never known my parents to be prejudiced, but then again, in the small town up north where I came from, there weren't many black people. Still, he'd never made negative comments about our black governor, at least not about the color of his skin. Was this part of his game? Or was he just trying to confuse me?

"Oh, stop it," I finally said. "What about you has ever been proper? You killed my mother!"

Papa's eyes welled with tears. "Is Karen dead? What happened? I've been waiting at this shitty hotel for her for days now." His demeanor turned sour. "I'm leaving. I've had it. Nobody tells me anything."

He got up and started to march to the door, but Bud, his guard, gripped Papa across the chest and slapped on handcuffs just as Papa tried to take a swing at him. He shoved Papa down in his chair. The other guard came over, and they cuffed Papa's legs. It took both of them because as Papa swung his torso, he also started kicking. Now he was yelling. "I want to see my lawyer!"

Two more guards came in, one of them motioned to me and Ric.

Papa raged as they led him away, but it looked like the guards were used to this behavior. So, had he been play-acting all this time, waiting for me to figure out he was behind the double homicide, my kidnapping, the videotaping of my suite?

Ric looked at his watch. "We had an appointment with the warden. Our visit with Mr. Van Slyke seems to have ended a bit early. Is Warden Denton available?"

Ric mentioned on the drive here he'd arranged for us to speak to the warden, and now I was more grateful than ever. If Papa had started acting like a mental patient a month or so ago, that would just be one more piece. Before Papa's act, I'd had a whole other set of questions, but now I just wanted to know how long this had been going on. I had no problem believing he had faked the scene for my benefit, but I'd never realized he was such a good actor. He'd been red in the face and spitting when we left, but his anger hadn't been directed at me. He seemed to have forgotten I was even there. Then there were the physical changes. My father had always been fastidious. Just now his hair had been messy, too long, and the facial hair had added to the general air of an unkempt old man.

The guard made a call and then led us upstairs two flights to another room with a clerk at a desk, who said, "He'll just be a few minutes, Detective Paxton. Ms. White."

We sat. "Ric. That was weird. I think he's faking."

"Do you…does your family have a history of Alzheimer's?"

I sucked in my breath. "Yes, but remote. A great-uncle on my father's side."

We talked with the warden, a very different conversation than I'd imagined. My father had been showing signs of dementia for two years although there hadn't been a formal diagnosis yet. My fault, I knew. I never took calls from the prison.

Warden Denton said a guard—"really just another inmate"—had been assigned when Papa started having episodes of angry outbursts. "He threw his lunch tray and said the chef should be fired." The warden shook his head. "Chef. Like we're some fancy resort."

I didn't know how to feel. He couldn't fake dementia for two years, could he? My all-but-solved puzzle had just been tossed back in the box and thoroughly shaken. What to do? My father was dead to me. I only resurrected him because I thought he was behind my kidnapping. I didn't want to be responsible for him, but he has no other surviving relatives.

"What's the protocol here?"

"It's sad," the warden said.

"No. He had my mother murdered."

"Well, yes, I understand, but in general, what we're up against here, it's a nightmare. Inmates will take advantage of someone in his condition. We can't have guards with him twenty-four/seven. We have a wing of the prison just for these cases."

"Wow. That's weird."

I knew I was supposed to show compassion, and I did feel a kind of horrified sorrow for the larger picture the warden painted of prison life, but I couldn't manage much sympathy for the guy who had killed my mother. His wife.

"So many lifers. It stands to reason some of them are going to get some form of dementia. You're lucky he's not in a state prison. Bit of a nightmare problem, there."

"Well. It's not my problem. I don't care what happens to him."

"Lily," Ric said, "he could be causing all kinds of havoc. It might be best to sign the paperwork and get him transferred to the care ward."

"It really is only a matter of you signing a release. He's been getting worse in the last six months."

"And you're sure he's not just faking it? So he can do easier time?"

"It's not easier. It's sadder. Gen pop has it pretty good in here, all things considered."

"Okay. Fine. Whatever." My mind went numb as the warden buzzed his secretary. She soon came in with a release form that I read and signed. "I'm done now. Correct?"

The warden seemed at a loss for words.

Ric was not. "Let's go, then, Lily."

Something about the softer way he said my name was like balm to my bruised heart. That and just not being alone or being with someone and wanting to be alone. That was gone. I wanted to be with Ric.

On the drive home, after I thought about it from every angle, I accepted the conclusion that it had not, in fact, been Papa who had plotted that stupid kidnapping. I'd been so sure. Over that period of three days, I had been certain I'd solved the mystery of the bedroom furniture. I'd been so sure Papa was the man behind it.

"Who else could have kidnapped me? And why?"

Ric patted my hand.

"I just don't get it. Nobody else has a motive." I thought furiously for a couple of minutes. This is more difficult to do with the remnants of a concussion than I would have imagined. "Unless…"

"What? Unless what?" Ric said.

I didn't get a chance to answer him because his

phone rang, and it was his mother. Inviting us to dinner. The minute I said yes to the invitation, I knew I loved him. There was no other reason I'd put myself through an interracial meet-the-family dinner.

Chapter 18

Lily

I admit it. I was so afraid to see Ric's family again. This time it would be for more than a brief introduction. What if, when they got to know me, they didn't like me? What if they sensed how close Ric and I were becoming? How could they not? So then what if they thought two white people in a black family was one too many? What if I said something stupid because I was nervous?

I have very few social skills. I cut right to the chase. It's always been that way and I know, because people have told me, actually people have screamed at me, that I am a selfish bitch. I don't think that's fair or true, but I've heard enough renditions of these kinds of comments to understand the way I see myself and the way the world sees me are not congruent. Ric sees me as I am, and that's one of the reasons I love him. And because I love him, I'm walking up the sweeping brick path to the Paxton's front door with him for Sunday dinner.

Palmer Park is a historic area of Detroit, a neighborhood full of gorgeous homes from a hundred years or so ago that have been kept up with love in every burnished piece of wood framing the doorway, in every brick swept and clean and every trimly clipped shrub. This is one of several safe and lovely neighborhoods that don't get the press or the photos like the wasted and ravaged formerly grand homes tend to do. I know this because I have been working with a Realtor since the day I left the hospital, and I'd seen those neighborhoods myself.

The chief opened the door himself just as our feet hit the porch. Ric squeezed my hand, and relief flooded through me. The chief was smiling. He gave his son a big hug and beamed at me, holding my free hand in both of his. "Come on in, you two."

Inside everything seemed to glow. Laughter mingled with delicious kitchen scents. Star was the first to greet us after the chief. She raised her arms to be picked up by Uncle Derrick and said, "Hey, Whitey!" to me. I was so surprised I laughed. Her sunny smile clearly showed she bore me no malice.

"Star," Ric's sister said. "It's Ms. White!"

"How about Lily?" I said to the family, who'd all set down their drinks and gotten up from sofas and chairs and moved into the large hall to greet us.

"Welcome, Lily," Ric's mom said, coming into the front hall from the kitchen, decked out in a designer summer dress and heels. For a grandmother, she had great legs.

"Thank you for including me," I said.

Honestly, the afternoon was a bit of a blur. Ric has three sisters and several nieces and nephews, all older than Star, all in attendance. Then there were the husbands. Star's white father blended into the general blur of all the beautiful shades we so inadequately call black. Not that I'd say that. In fact, I didn't say much, because I was so attuned to my own ability to say the wrong thing.

We gathered at the table after a young woman laid the last serving dish. "Does anyone need anything to drink?"

I'd decided not to drink any alcohol, even though just about everyone else of legal age had a glass of wine in front of them.

"We're fine for now. Just leave the bottle on the table and take a rest."

The young woman, maybe she was twenty or twenty-one, smiled and said, "Thanks, Chief."

Creating yet more commotion, dishes were passed every which way in no discernable order. I was impressed that all the plates matched, as did the chairs we sat on. And there were two dozen of us. No kids' table here. I'm not domestic, not really, even though Ric and I had been cooking and shopping together and it was fun. But that was for two people. Although Mrs. Paxton had help. I could hear the faint sound of pots and pans being rinsed from the kitchen.

I felt peppered with questions, but answering them was only awkward when I'd just taken a huge bite of tender pot roast or creamy potato. Mostly Ric's family, particularly the nephews, wanted to know about how it felt to be kidnapped. There'd been a news story on it, but I had declined an interview. I didn't even give the papers a quote.

"It felt like the longest exam ever," I said. "The never-ending exam from the class you despise the most." That got a laugh. I relaxed inch by inch.

Nobody asked about my family. I knew Ric had briefed them, and I silently thanked him for it.

"How do you like shacking up with my brother?" Shanita asked.

Maybe wine was called for after all.

"It's great," I said, proving that even sober I could be an idiot. "I mean, Ric has been so generous. But we aren't planning to live together long term. I've got a Realtor, and I'm close to signing a deal on a live/work space in the West Village."

Someone laughed. Then a few more laughs joined in.

"What?" I said, reaching for the wine bottle and pouring half a glass.

"Lot of white folks live there."

"Oh. I didn't know."

"Who's your Realtor?" Mama Paxton asked.

"Nate Slimvera." I hadn't chosen him because he was black. He was the first person I saw when I went to the real estate office, so I asked if he could help me. I took a sip of my wine and shot a quick look at the white guy down the table from me. I forgot his name, but I was sure he'd been one of the people laughing.

"Nate's the best," Ric said.

Nobody denied it.

Mrs. Paxton told her grandsons to quit horsing around and then said, "West Village is lovely. Its proximity to Indian Village will always give it a certain cachet."

"Your home is lovely. I like this neighborhood, and several others I've seen, but they are for families. I'm rebooting my business, and I want to work and live in the same building," I said.

"They're doing some of that in the West Village now," another brother-in-law, not the white one, said.

I nodded but felt like I needed to more directly address the race issue Ric's sister had brought up. I didn't want Ric's family to think I was looking for a white neighborhood. I hadn't known such a thing existed in Detroit. And despite her barb, I still wasn't convinced it was true.

"Nate and I don't talk about the racial mix of the neighborhoods. I've never asked, and he's never brought it up. I'm used to living with Iroquois and Chippewa at the casino, so…"

"Some very prominent people, judges and such, lived in the West Village back in the day." The chief deftly turned the subject to another angle.

I picked up my wine glass, Waterford crystal no less, and discovered it empty.

"Y'all are driving Lily to drink," Ric said, hefting the wine bottle and pouring me a generous glass.

This time I laughed with everyone else. Whatever tension had been in me broke, and I settled in for dessert with the Paxtons.

Later, after we were back at his place and sitting on the sofa with our feet up, Ric asked me about the house hunting. "You know you don't have to leave," he said. He'd said it before.

"I love you," I said, because I knew that was what his invitation to stay with him really meant.

He said he loved me, too, and we kissed. We held each other, there on the sofa, each with our own thoughts.

We'd talked about me staying on with him, using his guest room as an office space, but the fit just wasn't right. I needed more space for a huge project like filming the documentary that had been seeded in me at some point during my time in Detroit. A documentary that showcased the beauty I'd found here, and the damage. A film that showed glimpses of this pivotal moment in the city's history, when white people were moving back and co-existing with people of all colors. It was maybe too big a project, but once the idea sprouted, I knew I had to try. And I couldn't do it in Ric's place. I'd need staff. Equipment that couldn't be tucked discreetly into a few desk drawers at the end of the day.

"The other thing, I mean besides me needing the physical space for my work, is that I never have really lived alone. Someone is always just down the hall. At the casino, I had a kind of family. At least it felt that way to me. At college, I always had roommates. And where I came from…up north…there were people there I stayed with who loved me like one of their own. I was alone for a little while, but it was in a house they owned. I didn't pay rent. They constantly checked on me and brought me food."

"Family's important."

"Yours is great."

"I like them. And I could tell they like you."

"I hope so." I was thinking it would get easier every Sunday from now on. I'd memorize all the names and which kids and what man went with each sister. I'd stand my ground if I felt like I needed to, because everyone had seemed to respect that. After I'd responded to the remark about the West Village being full of white people, I felt like everybody, not just me, relaxed.

Now that the great hurdle of breaking bread with Ric's family had been jumped, I thought back to what

I'd been about to say when we got invited to dinner.

"Not trying to change the subject, but remember how I started to tell you about Eban Stern?"

"Eban Stern. Worked with Melanie and the vics in a small group trying to track a worm in Victory's computer system. You were looking for him when you were abducted."

"Yes. Remember I asked you if you could get a phone number, which was very wrong of me to try to use you that way, but I wasn't thinking about anything except finding Stern as fast as possible." My head hurt, memory rushed in so hard.

"So what was his motive for killing his co-workers?"

"I'm not sure. It had to be about that top-secret virus Kennedy told me about, the one that was internally planted and then so conveniently disappeared. I don't know what about all that would benefit Stern other than your usual sociopath messing with co-workers. But he has a motive for kidnapping me. He had tried to disappear. I got too close to finding him. He had me abducted."

"He didn't want to be found, so he put you in a room resembling to a remarkable degree your childhood bedroom." Ric's voice dripped irony.

"No, listen, this is not as far-fetched as Dan hiring a killer for his brother."

Ric patted my hand. "Sorry," he said. "Walk me through it."

"Okay. When you wouldn't get me the phone number—which of course I understand completely, we have to keep our boundaries tight—I did it the old-fashioned way. I called every Stern in the phone book.

Boring, but eventually I got a hit. Sort of. When I asked if Eban was home, this woman's voice changed. She said, "Who wants to know?" And then she hung up. I tried to call back, but she wasn't answering the phone. I thought about going out to the house—the address was in Birmingham—but then Jimmy called and demanded I talk to Dan, because he was afraid you guys were going to pin the murders on him. I figured I'd swing by the bar on my way to Birmingham."

"And you never made it to Birmingham."

"Nope. And…and there's more." My thoughts were clarifying almost too quickly. I'd been in an induced state of denial for days now, but that was over. "Stern knew I'd been tracking him. I'd found all sorts of red flags. He wanted me out of the way, but he's not a murderer. So he had me kidnapped."

"But the furniture, why go to those lengths?"

"Because it would divert me. If the knock on the head didn't do it, if being locked in a basement for three days didn't do it, then making me believe Papa was behind the whole thing from Roseann's murder on…it was a good plan. Solid psychopath scenario. Killing isn't his thing. Messing with the system, or somebody's head, that's his thing."

"Hmmm."

"Ric. I know it was him. He's probably long gone by now, but I need to warn Melanie."

"Okay, but wait. Why would he put cameras in your suite?"

"Maybe he did that first. To figure out how much I knew about him. To keep tabs. Maybe the videos going live online were an afterthought." My thoughts kept piling on, each rear-ending the one before. "Because the videos would just add to my thinking Papa was behind everything. I sent Papa to jail with a video. How like him to do the same to me."

"It seems a lot of work for not much payoff."

"Messing with somebody's head, messing with their life—there are certain kinds of sociopaths who live for games like that. The deep thrill when they successfully mess with someone or something is a huge motivator for a certain type of smart sociopath."

Ric was silent.

"Ric, this person knows all about me. Has looked at my ancient video channel. He tracked down furniture that matches my old stuff. Knows I have issues with panic. Has gone to some trouble to see me suffer. Sounds seriously sick."

"But not a murderer."

"Nope. But there are sick people who, you know—killing is not their kick. They like playing games with people. They like getting one over on somebody. They manipulate the system, be it at work—I found evidence of him playing the HR department at Victory—or like what he did to me. Anybody pisses them off, or doesn't give them proper respect, they love to get a good revenge. The setup is part of the fun for them. Anticipation. The thrill of the game is the only type of real feeling these sociopaths are wired for. They don't fall in love. They don't have friends. They might climb the corporate ladder, and many of them do, because they are ruthless, always, but mostly they love manipulating the system—any system—to make others look bad. And they are almost always male."

"Gee, thanks."

"Psychology 101. Just the facts."

"You don't think Jimmy fits that profile?"

"No. You saw him at the funeral. He loved his wife, in his strange way. He loves his family. And he's been paying me to find this guy. I must be close, and Stern figured it was time to mess with my head."

"Somebody did this to you. But are you sure it's Eban Stern? Yesterday, you were sure it was your father."

"Only because Stern wanted me to think that. He's the only one left. Well, Dan, but you know, that's full of holes."

"Let's say you're right. What did you do to disturb Stern?"

"I kept digging. Even when the police said they had a person of interest in custody. I didn't stop. He must have known I was looking at him. And I was the only one. The police were after Jimmy. Stern was videotaping my suite when I made those phone calls to every Stern in the book. And I got a hit on one. Maybe." I reminded Ric about the "who wants to know?" lady.

Ric nodded like finally, finally, he might be starting to really believe me, not just humor his slightly manic almost girlfriend.

"And where is this phone number?"

"On my laptop. With my files. Her name is Claire Stern."

"Your laptop is with LaRue in the tech lab." We were almost to Ric's place. "I'm going to drop you off and then go get that phone number and address. I'll go to Birmingham. You stay safe."

Once inside Ric's place, I tried to settle down. I paced, looking for a spot that fit. As I walked Ric's rooms, I thought about this profession I'd chosen. I'd never meant to involve myself with criminals or murderers or sociopaths. It was true, I did find missing persons for a living, but not dangerous ones. I found biological families for people who had been in foster care or adopted, relatives cut out of the family tree for a generation, husbands who left the state to avoid paying child support. I didn't help abusive husbands find the wife who escaped. I went out of my way to avoid those cases. Yet I'd taken Jimmy's case. Why? It was the videotaping. Missing persons don't require much video evidence. And I love shooting video. Definitely time for a career change.

I sat at the desk in the bedroom while I went through and replied to the business communications I'd missed with email and texts via my new phone. I wondered when I'd get my laptop back and if I should just buy another one. I left a message on my business line saying I was not currently taking on new clients. The truth was, I would never take on another client again. Not as a PI. But I did have to finish what I started. I had to find Stern. I had to clear my final client and his stoner brother of these crimes.

I went downstairs and plopped myself onto Ric's plush navy-blue sofa. I called Jimmy, and he answered the phone, loudly telling me off about his brother's arrest. Then he got control of himself and said, "I was sorry to hear about what happened to you. I bet if you'd been working the case instead of being held prisoner by some lunatic, Dan would not be in jail right now."

"Thanks for your faith in me, Jimmy."

"But it's not true, is it, that you're with Paxton now?"

"Yes. I'm staying at his place." I told him about the suite being compromised and about how I was convinced I now knew who'd hired the hits on Roseann and Kennedy. "It's a little tangled, but I'm unknotting as fast as I can."

"When will you be able to prove it?"

"Maybe today if you're finished telling me off." I smiled even though he couldn't see me. Jimmy laughed so he knew I was teasing. "You bond him out yet?"

"Working on it."

"It's a bogus charge, Jimmy."

"Does your boyfriend say so?"

"Detective Paxton is not saying either way."

Jimmy sighed loudly, so I promised he'd be the first to know when I caught up with the man who had hired a hit on his wife. We hung up, and I decided to get in a little time at the firing range. All these years, I'd kept guns because they made me feel safe. Yet, I'd only shot at a human target once. I didn't want to do that ever again. Convinced as I was that, while Stern had no problem hiring them, he wasn't a killer, I still wondered if he owned an unregistered gun. If he knew how to shoot it.

Before and then on the way to target practice, I called Melanie, leaving messages but hadn't heard back. At practice, I couldn't talk myself out of the dreadful feeling that Stern might come after Melanie next. Stern knew I had been doing some digging; that's why he had me kidnapped. But why all the video stuff? Ric was right to be skeptical. Even for a sociopath that seemed a bit much. I unloaded a full clip and reached into my bag for another. After reloading the Kimber, I pulled the target and was gratified to see that a few days off hadn't hurt my aim.

I headed over to Melanie's. On the way, I got a call from Ric. The woman who had briefly talked to me turned out to be Eban Stern's wife. She claimed she had no idea where he had gone; she hadn't seen him in two weeks.

"So she's looking for him too. She told me he'd cleaned out his office desk and bedroom drawers. Everything except the last three years of tax returns. 'He does all his banking and bill paying online,' the wife said. And of course his computer was gone. The wife had her own laptop, credit card, and bank account."

"Wow."

"Yes, but I only have her word for it. Husbands leave wives all the time."

"Buzz kill. But, yeah, I know."

"What have you been up to?" Ric asked.

"Talked to Jimmy; went to target practice; now I'm on my way to see Melanie."

"Be careful."

"Do you believe me about Stern now?"

"It's odd that he's disappeared. We'll see if they find his DNA in your suite. Whoever planted the cameras wore gloves, so no fingerprints. And LaRue is still looking at the cameras."

"I'm worried there's more video. Like with me naked." I finally spit it out. LaRue was a woman. I didn't mind her seeing the video. I just wanted to be sure Stern wasn't splicing it together for another international online video release.

"Stern has probably left town. You were too close to finding him, so he got you out of the way for a few days to put together an exit plan."

"Maybe." I couldn't help worrying about Melanie.

"Call me after you talk to Melanie."

"I'll text if there's a problem, but otherwise I'll see you at home."

"Don't worry about cooking. We'll order in."

I hadn't given the first thought to cooking, though I'd called Ric's place "home" without even thinking about it. I really needed my own place. It wasn't that I thought Ric was moving too fast; it was more like I might jump his bones if we spent another night in the same house. What would come after that? A subscription to *Brides* magazine?

I pulled into the parking structure for Melanie's building and went up to the third floor just as my phone buzzed. Melanie.

"Hey, I'm at your doorstep."

A door opened, and Melanie stepped out and waved. "Come on in," she said.

Melanie hadn't read the papers or watched the news so she had no idea about what had happened to me. After I gave her the highlights of the last couple of days, I spit out the real reason I was sitting across the kitchen table from her. "I think Eban Stern kidnapped me. I think he had Thomas and Roseann killed."

Melanie had been drinking a glass of water, and she crashed it down so hard on the table most of the water ended up outside the glass. "Shit," she said, reaching to grab a towel from the countertop. "Ugh." Melanie cradled her belly the way pregnant women did. I snagged the towel and mopped up the mess.

Melanie got up, still holding her belly, which had grown since I had last seen her, and refilled her water glass. "You sure you don't want anything?"

"No. I'm good."

"I take these allergy pills, and they make me so thirsty all I do is drink and pee."

A little alarm went off in my head. What was it? Something I was forgetting. Something important. Damn concussion.

"Your hair looks cute that way," Melanie said.

I noticed Melanie's long hair had a nice natural curl to it. Last time I'd seen Melanie, she'd definitely used a flat iron. So I lifted up my hair and showed the shaved area and butterfly bandage that my new side part hid.

"God!"

"I know. But listen, I've been thinking. You might not be safe. Stern knows I'm onto him. I suspect he's the one shooting me with hidden cameras and hiring hit men. Is there somewhere you can go?"

"He what? None of that sounds like Eban. He was so quiet. A real introvert."

"Well. He changes personas like we change hairstyles."

"What do you mean?"

"What if he's a sociopath? He could have tried some kind of sick revenge on me for looking into his life. Having me out of the way gave him time to figure out his next move. The videotapes might be like a mirror revenge. I spied on him, so he spied on me worse. I don't know." It sounded stupid when I said it out loud. Plus I still didn't know why he would have Roseann and Thomas killed. "My only reason for checking up on him was because he was in your group at Victory. It was basically checking him off my list.

But what should have been an hour's work turned into something else. It was like he's disappeared from the face of the earth."

"Well, maybe he just went on vacation."

"Not according to his wife."

"Eban's not married. I remember because we used to tease Roseann that she was the only married one on the team."

"Oh, he's married. He just lies a lot."

"What a jerk."

"More than that. One of the things I do is find missing people. I've found a lot of people. But he seems to have deliberately masked his personal information and erased or obscured any paper trail. Online, at work, even the home address he gave to HR was fake."

"But wouldn't they check that?"

"I'm sure he played the system somehow. Maybe changed the address after he was already inside."

"Jesus. Why would he do that?"

"Kicks." I was determined to talk Melanie into leaving town. I wanted her well away in case Stern was still watching me. It seemed like he'd want to exit town now that I was out of the makeshift jail cell he'd built for me, but I couldn't be sure. There was still a big missing piece: why had he had Roseann and Kennedy killed? I'm sure he knew suspicion would fall on my client, because "the husband did it" was default.

"Anyway. I found his wife. But before I could prove it, I got this." I pointed to the spot on my head where I'd been slammed. "And then I was abducted."

A fluffy white cat with black paws came into the room, sat at Melanie's feet, and meowed. Melanie got up and opened a can of tuna. "There you go, Your Highness."

We laughed.

"You won't believe what I have had to go through since Tom died. I can't clean out the litter box because I'm pregnant. Some kind of weird disease pregnant women can get from cat feces. Toxemia? Anyway, Tom always cleaned Gia's box. Then he died." Her eyes welled as she thought of all she'd lost. I knew that feeling. It's how I'd felt when my mom died. "So now I've hired the neighbor girl to come over and clean the cat box." She'd managed to sniff the tears back.

"If there's anything I can ever do, just let me know. I just bought a place close to here."

"Wow. Congrats. It's a great neighborhood."

"Yes, it is."

"It gives me chills to think Eban Stern set up your childhood bedroom to put you off his scent."

"It would not have been difficult for him to gain knowledge of my past. All those old videos on the Internet forever. He could have gotten the furniture from a simple eBay search."

"Do you really think I could be in danger?"

"I'm not sure, but I wish you could get out of town until we find him. The police are looking for him now. They have resources I don't." I wasn't sure that was true, about the police looking for Stern. I knew Ric was officially on vacation and unofficially helping me, but how much the department was involved—well, my story sounded out there, even to me, so I doubted Ric would try to convince anybody else of my conspiracy theory. He'd help me find proof, though.

"The police think Eban killed Tom? I thought they

arrested Roseann's brother-in-law?" Again, her hand went to her belly.

"Yes, well, the police want Stern for kidnapping and assault, not murder. Not yet. But the thing is why would Stern kidnap and assault me? It has to be because I was looking at him for my client. To help prove my client innocent of Roseann's death." I took a breath. I just needed a little more solid proof that Stern was the guy behind my abduction. And, of course, a way to connect him to the murders.

"I'm pretty sure he did it all. I just don't know why he had Roseann and Thomas killed."

Melanie shivered. "I can go up to Alaska for a visit. My mom keeps begging me to come home to have the baby."

"That would be good. Can you leave today?"

"I'd need to find somebody to cat-sit Gia, but I guess so." Melanie drank more water, and that's when it hit me. When I'd been at Kennedy's, hiding from a killer or his accomplice, the guy who'd come into the condo and wiped the computers had taken the time, even with the police on their way, to stop in the bathroom to get a drink of water.

"Do you know if Stern took medication that might make him thirsty?"

Melanie eyes flashed surprise. "How'd you know that? We used to bum them off each other this spring when everything in the city started to bloom."

"It's not important. And I can look after your cat. I'd be happy to do it."

"Really?"

"I, um, sure."

I was thinking about the allergy pills. The side

effect of thirst. It was a little piece of proof. Maybe the crime-scene techs could locate DNA that way. I quickly texted Ric, then I switched my attention back to Melanie. "Is it okay to take those when you're pregnant?"

"Yes, my doctor okayed the meds."

"Can you travel?"

"Sure. I'm only eighteen weeks."

I handed Melanie my phone. "Please give me your contact info in Alaska."

As she typed into my phone, I wondered why I cared so much. I didn't usually let myself get involved in the personal lives of clients or anyone connected with them. And yet, here I was, worrying over a pregnant woman like a mother hen.

Melanie handed me back the phone and pulled her own out. "I'll look up flights," she said. I was so happy she was taking me seriously. Even if I was being over-cautious, even if I had gotten it all wrong once again, I was still glad she was leaving town for a bit.

"There's a flight at seven o'clock tonight. I booked it. I better call my mom and warn her I'm coming. She doesn't have to know why I'm coming. She'll think I miss her, and she'll be thrilled."

I missed my own mother every day, so I knew what Melanie meant. "I feel like I should stay with you until you get on that plane."

"No, really, you don't have to! I need to call my mom, I need to pack, and then I'll get to the airport early. They're not going to let you through security, so you won't see me get on the plane." She smiled. "But it's sweet you want to."

"At least let me drive you to the airport."

"Okay. If you're sure."

Melanie had just finished packing when I got one of those news flashes on my phone. A1A had been hacked. Their system was compromised, and they would not be able to meet customer demand for their product for at least a month. Victory was their main client. As this news hit, A1A's stock immediately plunged. A1A. I knew that name.

On the way to the airport, Melanie fretted about her cat. I tried my best to assure her the cat would be fine between the sweet neighbor girl and my back-up care. I even texted the neighbor girl my number right then and wrote that she should call me any time she needed a hand with Melanie's cat.

"Okay?" I asked Melanie.

"Yeah, thanks. I know I'm being silly."

"Not at all," I said, thinking about the way people loved their pets.

After a few minutes, I asked Melanie about A1A. "Isn't that the supplier Stern was working with while everyone else on the team was tracking down the internal problem on Victory's computer system?"

"Yeah. I feel bad for them. Victory doesn't care. They'll get their parts from someone else."

"But eventually A1A will be able to run production again. Right?"

"Oh sure. I just don't know if Victory will switch back to them. I'm so glad I decided to take a long break from that place. It feels so far away. And I'm really getting excited to see my mom!"

I didn't say anything else to Melanie about A1A. I just told her to text me when she got on the plane and again when she landed.

She laughed and gave me a hug as I pulled up to the drop off curb for Alaska Airlines. Then she looked at me. "Do you think Eban had something to do with A1A? Like he could have written a malware program and set it on a delay?"

"Is it possible to do that? Write a program on delay?"

"Yes. He might have wanted some distance between when he was working with them and when their system crashed. But why would he do that? Just for fun?"

"I think this is the money part. He could buy up A1A stock in a short sale. Eventually, when the stock goes up again, he makes a juicy profit and hides it in an offshore account."

"Now the whole thing makes more sense."

"Just as well you're getting out of town. You don't need to worry about it."

"Well, if you crack the case, you better call me with all the details." She rubbed her belly. "He is the reason my baby doesn't have a father."

Chapter 19

Paxton

The airport was about twenty minutes outside the city. Paxton calculated Lily would have dropped Melanie off at four o'clock and was due back at his place by four-thirty. He was already home. Waiting. It was 4:43 before she walked in the door. She stopped just inside the door. Looked at him like she was startled to find him in his own living room.

"What?" Paxton said, walking closer. The sight of Lily, safe and whole, caused every molecule in him to move toward her.

"I know I bought a place of my own, but I'd feel better if we were together at night at least until Stern is behind bars."

"I like the way that sounds," he said.

"Or we can get a warrant, find Stern, and put him in jail." She explained about A1A and Victory and her short-sale theory. "Let's resolve this situation."

The intercom buzzed. Walter said he was bringing up the delivery.

"What delivery?" Lily asked.

"Pizza," Ric said.

"How did you know I skipped lunch?"

"I think we're on the same clock."

"And Walter doesn't even let the pizza guy come

upstairs? Impressive."

Soon they were sitting on the sofa, a bottle of wine open on the coffee table, eating pizza.

"Funny. You don't seem like the type of guy who eats pizza on the sofa."

"Why?" Ric took another slice.

"Your immaculate suits. Your impeccable hair." She ran her finger along the precise side part he paid a stylist to razor into his hair once a week.

Her touch made every fiber of his being stand up and take notice.

"Even your fingernails look like you have a personal manicurist on speed dial."

He laughed. "No manicurist. Just a mom who insisted on excellent personal hygiene."

She laughed, then started talking about A1A, ending with "There's your motive."

"I saw the A1A story," he said. "Need you to fill out that part about a motive a little more."

"Okay. I know DNA takes a long time to process. But you said they are working on the faucets from Kennedy's place and from mine, now, too."

"Yes, if they find DNA, which is going to be difficult, because we're talking running water, a mouth without much saliva, and a careful criminal who probably sipped from mid-stream, not the nozzle of the faucet."

"Right, yeah, so probably won't get DNA to prove Stern is the mastermind behind two murders and a kidnapping."

"We live in hope."

"Okay, but also…let's see if we can pick through this thing for some other kind of proof."

"A1A?" Ric had a feeling Lily had developed another theory.

"A1A was Stern's project while the other three on the Victory team chased down the signature of whoever planted the virus on their software. Melanie told me that at Kennedy's funeral. Stern had offered to take care of A1A while they did the internal search. But what if Stern was only working at Victory so he could sabotage A1A? What if he planted the mysteriously vanished virus into Victory's system so the team would be chasing a false lead, so he could offer to babysit A1A, which Melanie said was the kind of vendor who needed a lot of tech support, and then Stern finally inserted a kind of delayed malware into A1A, which Melanie says he could have absolutely done, and deleted the Victory virus, but he'd only managed that after Roseann had found his signature? What if Roseann was taking her knowledge directly to Kennedy because she distrusted Stern to the point that she didn't want to use the phone or computer?"

"Why wouldn't she text Kennedy that info from her own phone?" Paxton decided Lily was either brilliant or had a vivid inner life. Maybe both.

"I don't know. I'm not sure how the signature thing works. Maybe, just say, she freaked when she found out Stern was the person responsible for the virus. She took a screenshot and mailed it to herself, then erased her history and closed down the computer. It's Friday night. Late. And Stern is still working or pretending to— because now she knows it's him. And he's there. She doesn't want to send anything out; she doesn't want to stay at work with Stern a second longer; she has to see Kennedy in person. Show him the screenshot on her phone."

"So she goes to his apartment," Paxton said, "and Bingo follows her."

"Stern calls Bingo…" Lily continued.

"So Stern is the one who hired Bingo?"

"Yep." Lily went on. "Bingo relays their whereabouts. Stern suspects Roseann found the signature. He can delete the whole virus and thus the signature from Victory's system, but it's too late if Roseann has a screenshot or some other type of proof of the signature. Stern knows this and offers Bingo extra incentive to execute Roseann."

"It fits. We never found Roseann's phone, and all Kennedy's electronics were wiped before we got there."

They looked at each other then, the significance of Roseann's missing phone not being lost on either one of them.

"You were rolling tape when Roseann was shot," Paxton said.

"Yes. And I dropped the camera into the glove box, took out my Sig, and ran over to Roseann."

"So Bingo got her phone in those seconds when you were retrieving your weapon."

"It had to be. He was nowhere in sight as I ran up to the building. Nobody shot at me."

"But then. After you called 9-1-1, before I arrived, you went into a fugue."

"I did."

"So he could have waited and grabbed the phone after you called 9-1-1."

"Yes." She put her head down. It hurt her to admit this.

"It's not your fault. I think he probably grabbed the

phone before you ran up to Roseann. He knew someone would call 9-1-1. He wasn't going to hang around." Paxton didn't think about it, he just put his arm around Lily. "I wonder what Bingo did with that phone," he said.

Lily seemed to perk up even as she leaned into his one-armed embrace. "That would have the screenshot on it. I mean, if Roseann really did take one."

"Unless whoever hired Bingo told him to destroy the phone. Or arranged to confiscate it."

Lily sat up straight, and Paxton let his arm drop away. "Bingo didn't make bail."

"No, he did not."

Lily nodded, on a roll. "What if Stern planned all of this as a long game? You know how I said his profile fits the guy who loves the long game? The final outcome is A1A's stock crash, with time for Stern to cash in on a short sale and leave town. That would explain why he planned my kidnapping so meticulously, too. He was bored. Waiting for phase one of his plan to end successfully. Waiting is not the favorite part of the game this type of sociopath plays, but sometimes it's necessary. So messing with my head was just a cheap thrill on the side. Something to do while he waited to cash in on that devalued stock."

"You make a compelling argument," Paxton said. He wasn't as enthralled with the short sale theory as she wanted him to be, but the possibility of that phone made his heart pound. "It's unfortunate there's no evidence to support your story." She was connecting invisible dots, but you could say the same about his own PD for arresting Dan Heyl. He needed to question Bingo about that phone.

"Well, but maybe there will be. Evidence."

"Possibly." Paxton knew that phone could be anywhere now. "You do know short sales are legal?"

"Yes, I did a little research. He can also have set up an off-shore account under a dummy corporation and have the funds from the short sale wired directly there."

And there she goes again. "Then it's not a local police matter anymore."

"Well, but—" She set down her plate, the slice half finished. "There's still A1A. Can't LaRue look into the malware? Might that somehow lead to Stern?"

Paxton thought Lily might be on to something, but before he could tell her so, his phone rang. Headquarters. He picked up. Listened for a few minutes. Said thanks. Clicked off and put his phone in his pocket.

"Crime-scene folks are finished with your suite. You can go back now." He watched her carefully. Her face was impassive, but her hands clenched. He couldn't help it. He reached out and took both her fists into his, and she relaxed her fingers until they entwined with his. "But I wish you'd stay."

"Why?" She turned her head so he didn't see her face. "Stern isn't violent. Even if he's still following me, he's not stupid enough to show himself. More likely he's sunning himself on a beach somewhere waiting for his cash to roll in."

Paxton pulled Lily close. She refused to look at him, closing her eyes as she turned toward him. Before she put her head against his chest, a tear escaped and ran down her face. She ignored it. He wanted to kiss her then. She tried to be so tough, and she was so hard on herself. Lord only knew why his usual resistance

212

melted as his thumb brushed the tear from her cheek and his lips found a sweet spot just above her eyebrow. He kissed her there, allowed himself a brief lapse before he stepped away.

"I'm sorry. I have to go. That was Nigel. There's been a break in your abduction case."

"But—? That's not your case."

He didn't want to tell her what was happening with Franklin Roosevelt Jones, but he wanted to tell her something. To make her stay. "Stern is not on a beach right now. He's here, in town. Please, Lily, just stay here tonight."

"Okay…wait. How do you know Stern's still in town?"

He couldn't read her face, but he knew how her mind worked. She wasn't going to stay put. Dan Heyl had also made bail today and she'd be thinking about him, about how she needed to prove that neither Dan nor Jimmy had done the crimes his department had pinned on Dan. Her own safety wasn't making any impact.

"I can't talk about it. Please stay here where you're safe. I need to go, but I can't leave unless you promise you'll stay right here."

"It's still early. Look." She nodded toward the windows. "Daylight."

"You've got about two hours of daylight left."

"I need a meeting with my client and his brother. I've lain low here with you for a few days, even though there are things I could be doing to prove Dan's arrest was bogus. I mean, yes, he needs to close down his side job and probably go to rehab, but Dan did not hire anyone to murder Jimmy's wife. Or Kennedy."

"What are you going to do?"

"I want to find Diablo's storefront and interview him and his employees. I want to look at their closed-circuit cameras and ID every person who does business there. Then I want to question them, too. Somebody did the cash drop-offs for Stern. It can't be a coincidence that the money both my kidnappers and Bingo received was sent from the same location. If one person did both cash drop-offs, I'll find that person and maybe they can ID Stern. At some point, Stern had to hand over cash to somebody."

Paxton didn't want to argue with Lily. She was right. Someone in this little band of bozos had likely seen Stern.

"Lily, please don't. We're working on that. You'd be interfering with our investigation. Believe me, we will get the person who conveyed the cash for Stern. And if it turns out this person can ID Stern, we'll find that out, too."

"Didn't you try that before you arrested Dan Heyl?"

"Yes. Dead end. But we have a new lead."

"What? Who?"

"I can't say anymore. I shouldn't have told you what I did. Your instincts are good, baby. They're too good. But please, please, don't go there. Be patient. Let the wheels of justice work."

"Ha." She laughed, just a short fake bark of a laugh. "One of your wheels has a flat." Then she sighed. "I trust you, and I don't want to make this mess any worse than it already is, so I'll stay out of it."

"Thank you."

It wasn't until he was halfway to headquarters that

he realized she'd never said she'd stay safe at his place.

Chapter 20

Lily

I was glad Ric didn't want me to go to the casino or even stay at Melanie's. It proved he cared. I didn't particularly want to go to the hotel either, but I always faced my fears. And what exactly did I have to fear at the Iroquois?

That Stern was still tracking me? How likely was that? He'd had his big win today with A1A's market share bottoming out. He'd likely scooped up the sharply discounted stocks, but they hadn't paid out the big money yet. That would only come when the price rose again. Still, what could he possibly want with me now? I'd served my purpose. If Ric was right and Stern was still in town, well, he was not as smart as I thought. He'd pulled off his long game and even enjoyed a little side action. Why in the world was he still here?

I didn't want to waste time thinking about Stern, but one thing still bothered me. Was there any more footage of me out there? Was there anything in the suite I still wanted before I checked out permanently? I wanted my jewelry. I didn't have much, but Stern wouldn't have touched the good stuff I kept in the hotel safe. And who at the casino had let Stern into my suite in the first place? I wanted to question a few people.

Remembering I had not promised Ric to stay away

from the Iroquois, I headed out. He had his job and I had mine.

****

The hotel registration desk was empty. Unusual. I went down the back corridor to the offices. All the nine-to-five workers were gone, but the night manager, Jacinda, sat at her desk watching a split video screen.

"Hey," I said.

"You're back! I heard they released your room. Welcome home."

"Thanks. Nobody's at the front desk. Could you get my jewelry out of the safe?"

"That's weird...about the front desk, not your jewelry. I'll get it right away."

She left and returned with my velvet-lined box. My mom had used this leather jewelry box for travel. It had her monogram stamped in gold in the center of the modest-sized box. I was so happy to have it back, I held it for a minute before opening it. Then I took a quick peek. I had about a dozen pieces made of rose gold, my favorite precious metal. I loved rubies, so many of the items featured the gemstone. My favorite was a ring and necklace my mother had designed for me when I graduated college. It was the last gift she'd ever given to me, and that fact was more precious than any jewel. I clicked the box shut and stuffed it in my purse right on top of my Kimber.

"Who's on shift tonight?"

"Brad."

She clicked the video screen on her desk. Brad was back at his post.

"Okay. Thanks, Jacinda." I started to leave. "One more thing."

"Sure, Lily, whatever I can do to help."

"Do you know who on staff allowed someone to enter my suite?"

"No. Housekeeping, but that's routine. The police have questioned everyone. None of us know how your security was breached, but we have made you new key cards with a stronger passcode."

I knew someone on staff had let Stern into my suite, but of course nobody was going to admit to it.

"Hey, Brad," I said, coming out from the office corridor.

"Hi! We're all so glad you're safe," he said.

"Thanks."

"Here's your mail." He handed me a small bundle of envelopes. I stuffed those in my purse, too. I closed the purse, then opened it again, placing the Kimber on top of the mail and the jewelry box. I hadn't had time to get a special pouch made for this purse. Maybe I'd take a few of my favorites.

"I understand I have new key cards."

"Oh, right. Sorry." He reached under the desk and handed me the cards.

"Thanks, Brad."

"Anything for you, Lily."

That's what they all say until they take a bribe to let somebody into your suite. Well, it's not like I would be staying here anymore. I can't believe I'd once felt so secure here. What a joke.

I took the elevator up and caught housekeeping just leaving my suite. The door was ajar, and the cleaner seemed to be speaking to someone inside the room.

"Excuse me? Is someone in my rooms?"

The woman looked unfamiliar, but that wasn't

unusual. I never used night housekeeping. Room service, sure. But housekeeping came every morning at ten a.m. My door closed with what should have been a satisfying click. The housekeeper smiled wide, and her eyes twinkled. "Someone is very fond of you," she said. "Lucky girl."

"What are you talking about?" I unzipped my purse and put my hand on the Kimber, leaving it inside the bag but ready to rip out at a moment's notice.

"Someone left you flowers. I was just delivering them."

Brad hadn't mentioned any flower delivery.

"Thanks," I said. "But who were you talking to when I came up just now?"

She blushed. "I talk to myself sometimes. Silly habit."

She was young, maybe a college student working nights. She seemed harmless, but something felt off. I watched her walk down the hall and into the elevator before I pulled out my weapon. I had my key card in one hand and my gun in the other. I opened the door, dropped the key card into my purse, and wrapped my hand more securely around the grip of my weapon. I opened my door with one foot, tossing my purse inside before entering. Then I put my finger on the trigger and eased the door slowly open.

He was waiting for me. He must have paid that stupid girl a very large tip. With my free hand, I reached into my back pocket for my phone.

"I just want to talk," Stern said.

Funny, I wanted to talk too. "What the hell were you doing with that furniture and kidnapping me? You might have got away with everything if you hadn't played that game."

"I'll still get away. And it was fun. You shouldn't have interfered. I was paying you back."

"Why not just have another Bingo kill me?"

"Where's the fun in that? I'd been watching your videos and thought it would be a neat trick to turn the cameras on you for a change."

"My bedroom? The furniture?"

"That wasn't difficult. eBay. A friend owns the store. Never asked why he had an empty cell in the basement."

I kept the Kimber trained on center mass as I pressed speed dial while bringing my phone out of my pocket. Ric didn't answer. "Stern is here at the Iroquois with me," I said, dropping the phone on top of my purse and put both hands around the barrel of the Kimber.

Stern was shaking his head as if it was a damn shame I'd been so rude. He stood, and I moved away from the door, keeping the Kimber on him. He hadn't been violent up to this point, but I wasn't taking any chances.

"I'm leaving now. I thought we could talk about the rest of the video I have of you. This one I just put together is X-rated, I'm afraid. Was going to offer it to you for a good price."

He was out the open door with his last words. I still had the Kimber trained on his back. I held it with two hands, so I wouldn't shake with the fury I felt. As he had passed me, part of me wanted to shoot him in the foot or the shoulder, anything to incapacitate him, to hold him until Ric could get here. Instead, I followed him down the hall to the service elevator. My phone started to ring from the room. I kept the Kimber trained on Stern as I stepped into the elevator with him. I ignored the phone. Nothing I could do about it now. Neither one of us said a word on the ride down.

The service elevator opened to a large room with industrial washing machines and shelves of white towels. The girl who'd been in my room was stocking a laundry cart with soap, chatting with another woman who folded towels. They looked shocked as we stepped off the elevator. Stern walked right past me and my Kimber and kept going out the swinging door into a corridor of the hotel I'd never had reason to visit. He kept walking, and I followed him, keeping a couple steps behind.

He'd taken maybe three or four steps when he stopped and turned toward me. "We can still make a deal."

"I doubt that," I said. I thought about trying to engage him until Ric or someone arrived to arrest this guy, but by the time I'd finished the thought, hotel security had arrived.

There were two security guards, one had his weapon on me, the other on Stern. "What's the problem here, Ms. White?"

"This man, Eban Stern, was in my room. One of the staff let him in. My room was a crime scene until a few hours ago because this guy got in before. The minute I'm cleared to come back to my home, I find him sitting there. You people need to do your jobs."

"We're aware of the situation, Ms. White."

One of the guards moved to detain Stern, but Stern shook the guy off.

"This is all a misunderstanding," Stern said, stepping away from the security guards. "I was just dropping off flowers, and the housekeeper said it would be fine if I waited for Ms. White. No crime has been committed here." Stern kept walking right past me toward an emergency exit at the end of the corridor. I bit my lip to stop from shooting him. I wouldn't like myself much if I shot an unarmed man in the back. Then he opened the emergency exit door, sounding the alarm.

"You need to detain him until the police arrive," I yelled over the alarm. "He just tried to blackmail me." The guards just stood there as Stern walked free. I went outside after him. It had been all of thirty seconds since he'd left the building. But he had disappeared. It was just dusk, so I swung my eyes around the back lot. People were streaming out of every exit and a few people screamed when they saw me pointing a gun at thin air. I tucked the Kimber into the back of my jeans and went after a car from the employee lot that suddenly roared to life. But I was too late. Stern sped around the building, heading toward the exit onto Jefferson.

I ran after him anyway. I considered shooting his tires out but didn't want any bullets hitting the concrete and ricocheting into the crowds of panicked people. I memorized the license plate number. Because I kept up my pursuit, I witnessed, with not a little bit of sweet triumph, several Detroit police cars covering the exits.

Chapter 21

Paxton

Franklin Roosevelt Jones sat across from Paxton and Nigel in a plain smallish room at headquarters. This room was used to interview people who were not suspects or persons of interest in any crime, so the chairs were nicer and the table didn't have a handcuff link bolted to it. There was no tape rolling. No recordings of any sort except Paxton's pen and notebook. There was a door to a hallway that led to a back lot for complete secrecy when needed.

Paxton needed secrecy now. His gaze landing on the large bundle of bloody gauze bandages piled into the middle of the table. The blood was fake.

"You've been in jail for forty-eight hours. Long enough?" Paxton asked.

"Should be," Jones replied. "You kept your part?"

"Nobody except the people in this room know you were not the person who assaulted Lily White."

"Not even the chief?" Jones said.

"We'll be reading him in after this meeting. It won't be a problem." Paxton hoped that was true.

Paxton and Jones went way back. They'd been at the same private school in Detroit but had parted ways when Jones got accepted on a basketball scholarship to Duke. Jones graduated with honors but didn't receive any offers to play basketball professionally. Paxton and his family had attended Jones's homecoming party at the Yacht Club. Then, much to the consternation of his family, Jones joined the FBI, going deep undercover in one of the most notorious gangs in Detroit. The Diablos.

Interviewing Twitch Eye, Paxton had slipped Jones's photo into a book of mug shots. He made sure Jones was surrounded by plenty of white low-life types. Twitch Eye had picked out Jones right away as his accomplice, as Paxton figured he would. The only description Twitch Eye had given before looking at the mug shots was "blacker than you and taller, too." That description fit Jones as far as it goes, but it fit another criminal, too. Diablo.

Jones was a member of Diablo's crew and had come forward when word came down that there was an APB for a "tall black male" and offered to take the fall for an assault the top wolf in his pack had committed. Diablo had received the sacrifice as his due. He had other important gang business to attend to, if Jones would do the time for him. A deuce at most, Diablo said. He and the club would be gratified.

"It was good news all around," Jones told Nigel and Paxton. "I had skirted away from doing any real harm in the community for too long. If I'd do time for Diablo, that would be the ultimate proof I was loyal."

"And now you've paid the ultimate price for your loyalty." Paxton had been gratified the fake stabbing had gone according to plan, and he'd notified Jones's family of what had truly gone down before photos and videos of a beaten, bloody Jones had been posted all over the Internet. After the chief approved the op, the

DPD would put out a statement that Jones had died from his wounds. Sometimes fake news was good.

"We've appreciated the heads-up you've given us thus far, but this is big," Paxton said. "Bigger than anybody knows." He went on to tell his partners they were looking at Diablo as a link to a double homicide.

"Not the Heyl case? I thought y'all had a solve on that." Jones looked thoughtful.

"It won't stick. It was a great headline, though," Nigel remarked.

"What about the chief?" Jones persisted.

"Nigel and I have a meeting with him scheduled in thirty minutes."

"Nobody except my family knows I'm undercover. Not the force, not even the chief," Jones said.

"I love you, Rosie, but I wasn't sure you'd make it out of Diablo's team alive," Paxton said.

"Or straight," Franklin Roosevelt Jones answered with an easy grin.

"Paxton will do right by you. I'd pestered him for two years to move up the chain and then one day, it happened," Nigel said.

"It will be a little different for Rosie," Paxton said. "He won't be staying in Detroit. He'll be moving to an undisclosed location. Rosie's a Fed."

"No shit? I thought he was your CI," Nigel said.

"Yeah, well, Rosie and I made a promise before he went into Diablo's lair. It was just the two of us. So, I had to tell you something, but I had to keep it down low until Rosie got his new assignment."

"But you'd think your dad—"

"It was a take-it-or-leave-it kind of offer," Paxton said. What made Rosie's work so safe was the fact that even his family, except his parents, thought he'd gone over to the bad side. Now that he was moving from Detroit, he might be able to tell his siblings he was still alive and working for the government. But for Paxton's part of the plan to work, they had to tell the chief. And soon. Paxton's phone buzzed in his pocket, but he didn't look at it. One step at a time.

Rosie talked, and Paxton took notes. When they were finished, Paxton shook Rosie's hand, and Rosie pulled him in for an arm bump and slap on the back. Nigel escorted Rosie out to an unmarked car with tinted windows far in the back lot, where, his part done, he was whisked away to places unknown.

****

"I always liked Roosevelt Jones," the chief said.

"He's helped us out, for sure," Paxton admitted. "Lily couldn't find any hard evidence against Stern until Rosie gave us a lead." He didn't say that the department had been totally off course chasing the Heyl brothers.

"Sharing Diablo's second set of books answered many questions."

"We're serving arrest warrants by the dozens." Paxton relaxed in relief. His father, even after being kept in the dark about Rosie until recently, was on his side.

He'd hit the highlights of the debrief with Rosie for his dad and explained the curious set of circumstances that led Paxton to work with his old buddy again. Bingo's assault weapon was of military grade caliber, and there was only one criminal in Detroit known to have this particular weapon and model. Diablo. At the time, they had Bingo in jail with no out, so the gun was just a courtesy text to Rosie. Then Lily was kidnapped. Still, it wasn't until Twitch Eye had said a black man was his accomplice that Paxton got in closer touch. He and Rosie worked out a complicated bust that involved several local and federal agencies. Deep in the details, Rosie said it was known within the crew that Bingo had been hired by Stern to hit Roseann Heyl and Thomas Kennedy.

They'd figured out they could take Diablo's crew down for gunrunning and money laundering as well as running a ring of murders-for-hire. Once they got Diablo and some of the top-level crew on charges, Rosie stood up to do the time for his leader. Then Rosie's staged stabbing happened in county jail.

His dad nodded. "Proud of your work, son." Then he paused. "I'm sorry about Lily."

"Lily?" What? He remembered his phone had been on silent but buzzed while he and Rosie had played out their plan.

He pulled out his phone and clicked voicemail. His stomach twisted. Lily had needed him, and he hadn't been there for her. He felt a stab to his gut before his father spoke again.

"No worries," Dad said. "She's fine. In fact, she got Stern. Went to her suite at the Iroquois, and he was waiting there for her. Tried to blackmail her for videotape. With the heat on Diablo, he needed money until his short sale pays off. She didn't fall for it. She was ready to take him down with that pistol of hers but says he was unarmed, so all she could do was chase him through the hotel and force him out an emergency exit, which rang alarms and alerted hotel personnel, who called us."

"I thought LaRue said she'd disabled the feed. Or whatever it is she does so Stern can no longer upload the content from those tapes."

"She did, but Lily didn't know that. She thought he had all manner of new video exposing her in all her glory. She followed him out to his car, got video of his license, and luckily, we had the downtown precinct in place in record time. You can tell her 'good work' when you see her."

Paxton barely heard his father's words. "Where is she?"

"I think she's giving her statement at the downtown precinct."

"Okay, thanks, I have to go."

"We expect you two at dinner on Sunday."

Paxton nodded and shook his father's hand. Then he called downtown and asked to speak to Lily.

"She just left. We got her statement."

"Thanks," Paxton said. He didn't ask where she'd gone. He had a feeling he knew.

****

"Hey, baby," Paxton said.

"Say, you look like you just solved a crime," Lily said.

"That makes us even, right?" They both laughed.

"Cocktails with story swaps?"

"You bet," she answered.

Paxton was finished with giving a shit about anything other than loving this woman, every inch of her, inside and out. He even loved the air around her, especially when it included him. They had much to discuss.

"Let's have vodka in these cute martini glasses,"

she said, taking two out of the cabinet full of crystal drinkware his mother and sisters had surprised him with as a "divorce gift."

"Blue cheese olives?"

"Hmm." Lily thought. "I bought a block of gorgonzola at Whole Foods. And I bought olives." She took these things out of the fridge; he found the cocktail shaker and filled it with ice.

His standard procedure: Fill the shaker with ice. Pour vodka until it brimmed up to the ice. Add a mere jot of dry vermouth. Shake. This time he decided to stir. What the hell.

He watched Lily remove pimentos from large olives with a toothpick and then hand stuff six of them.

"Cocktail time," she said. "Sip and spill."

"Why don't you go first?"

"Because you probably read the report before you got home."

"This is true."

"Here's one thing." She sipped her martini and set it on the coffee table. "I was livid when they carted him away, and I demanded to see the housekeeping woman who'd been leaving my suite when I arrived. I knew she must have let him in."

"This was not in the report."

"You can add it tomorrow. I didn't want to get her fired, but I was so pissed, especially when she said she'd let him in twice. Once on the day he put in his cameras and then today. You want to hear her reason?"

"I want to put her in jail."

"That won't be necessary. I scared the crap out of her, and she's young and we all do stupid things when we're young. Well, maybe not you." Lily tucked her feet under her legs. "So, she said she felt sorry for him. He told her these sob stories about how we'd been separated for months because of his work and he wanted to leave me a gift. That was the first time."

"He gift-wrapped the cameras he installed to spy on you."

They laughed and exchanged a look. It felt to Paxton like their eyes did something more than see each other. They connected. Tight as two loose strings making a strong knot.

"Yes. And then today he brought flowers. He said we'd had an awful time of it with my room being broken into, and he needed to be there to surprise me and make me feel safe. 'Give a heartsick guy a break' were his words." She picked up her drink and took a swallow. "This is good," she said. "I feel the vodka."

"So how'd he know you'd be there?"

"I didn't think about that until I was on the way home, um, here."

Paxton drained his martini glass. "Home is here," he said, "if you want it."

She slid one of her legs out from under her and wiggled it under his thigh. "We have a ways to go, don't we?"

But the way she said it made it clear she was in this with him. He was not feeling the love alone. He took her bare foot and began to massage it, rubbing the arch and the heel and smoothing his fingers over her toes. "So, how'd he know?"

"If you think about it, you'll be able to solve that one before I finish my drink." She sipped. "That feels so good," she said, pulling her other foot out from under her and sliding it his way.

"I'd say our security spotted him too close to the building, parked in his car overlong, kept an eye, and when you came out of the apartment, saw him follow you," Paxton said.

"Yep," Lily said.

"So we have the tape if we need it. I guess that depends on what you tell me."

By this time, he'd started working out the stress points of her other foot. She made soft sounds of pleasure.

"My God, where'd you learn to do that?"

"Reflexology book."

"Hmmm. It's better than vodka."

"You want a refill?"

"I want Chinese food. I forgot to eat today."

"What about the pizza earlier?"

"Look at your watch."

He did. It was after midnight. Okay, so pizza was yesterday.

She was already on her phone, ordering a string of dishes, all their favorites. When it occurred to him they already had their favorites, their habits and routines, it made him happy and a little afraid.

"I think I have a bottle of sake."

"You would." But she said it like he was a miracle worker, not some wine snob.

"You'll recall I have three sisters. And there's my mom. They have this idea that every time they visit, they have to bring food and gifts and things."

"Your family's so solid."

He sighed. "It took a long time for our family to get here. We didn't come up easy." He stopped there. She didn't need to know, or maybe he gave her credit for already knowing, how hard black boys and men not born with privilege or wealth had it in these United States. Their children would have it easier because of what his father and mother, his grandparents and their parents, too, had sacrificed. Their children. Was he already thinking that way? They hadn't even shared the same bed yet. *Boy, you got it bad*, he thought.

Lily didn't say anything, but she tucked her feet under her so that she was kneeling on the sofa. She put her arms around Paxton and leaned in for a hug. Then she turned slightly, settling in on his lap. She kissed him first. He pulled her closer and kissed her for a long time. He was determined to get it right. It felt right to him. "I'm sorry," she said. "More inadequate words were never spoken."

He nodded, thinking she hadn't had an easy life, either. "We have family dinner on Sunday. Every Sunday."

She nodded. "I know."

"Okay, now what happened at the station?"

He told her as little as possible about Roosevelt Jones. "Friend of mine from back in the day. He'd been undercover with a street gang dealing in murder-for-hire, assault weapons sales, money laundering, drugs, you name it. I knew, but nobody else in town had a clue. Lots of kids who look promising in school fall short in the world. I went to him when you said you were going to the storefront to find out if there was a connection between Bingo and Stern's money transfers. That storefront belongs to Diablo. I knew Diablo was the big fish the FBI wanted. Rosie did me a favor and sent me a copy of the second set of books."

"What about the guy on the news? The one killed

in jail?"

"When we busted Twitch Eye, he fingered a black man as his accomplice." He told her how he'd inserted Rosie's picture into a page of white faces.

"So your friend was killed?"

"No. Movie trick. So Diablo believed Rosie was dead. He's been reassigned. This is for your ears only." He realized he'd probably said too much, but he trusted her.

"Why would a drug and arms dealer do a kidnapping?"

"When Bingo did the hits on Roseann and Kennedy, he was promised big payment, which he never received. He yelled about it, and Diablo decided to find out exactly who had stiffed his soldier. There's a network of passing the money along the pipeline for those too shy to show their face at the store. But Diablo convinced Stern's cash jockey to set a meeting. Stern said since Bingo was in jail, he wouldn't need the money. Diablo thought that was hilarious. Stern paid Diablo's cut and asked the cost of grabbing you. Asked about a safe place to stash you. Said he was playing a head game, paying you back for interfering with his work."

Just then the house phone rang. Walter called to say their food order had arrived and did they want it sent up or would they come down? They were one guard short, as a statement was being given to the police. "I'll go," Lily said.

Just as Lily returned with the food, Paxton found the sake but was amazed to discover the female members of his clan had not yet gifted him with a little set of ceramic cups.

"I'll have water," Lily said. She took two glasses from a cabinet and filled them.

It touched Paxton that she knew he liked a slice of lemon in his water and that he too would prefer it to Japanese wine with Chinese food. He'd put big spoons in the cartons, and Lily took the waxed paper bag that held their egg rolls. She ate hers with her fingers, biting off the top and pouring the sauce down inside the egg roll as Paxton related the last nail in Stern's coffin.

Lily jumped up and washed her hands. "I've got to call Jimmy! It's finally over, thanks to you." She kissed Paxton and ran upstairs. He sat with five or six open containers of Chinese food, not thinking about food at all. He closed up the containers and wondered if she was off the phone yet. He went upstairs and headed to her room. On the way, he saw her sprawled on his bed.

"I love the king size," she said. "And this duvet is so soft."

"You know, you're welcome in my bed anytime. There's just one condition." He walked in the room and sat down next to her on the bed.

"What's that?" She scooted toward him.

"I can show you better than tell it," he said.

Then he proceeded to do just that.

Chapter 22

Lily

Ric was standing in the living room, wearing blue jeans and a white shirt, his feet bare. He was watching a news report. I kicked off my own shoes and walked to where he stood. Same reporting about the case we had worked on together. I sat on the sofa and paid attention. There might be a new detail or two. Ric came and sat beside me. We shared one of our increasingly intense looks and a kiss before turning back to the news program. The case, or at least the part of it that I'd been involved in, had been covered endlessly from every angle on the local news, and yet, here again was another iteration, complete with backstory. I put my head on Ric's shoulder, and he laid his hand on my hair where my head wound was finally healing. We let the old information sink in, wondering what new tidbit the media might add.

The old news was that my client had been exonerated, and the charges against his brother had been dropped. Eban Stern had been charged with double homicide and kidnapping. His request for bail had been denied and so had that of his accomplices, at least the ones still alive. The "pills and wine" video of me flashed across the screen, and I winced. Whenever the news channels could figure out how to slip that video into the reports, they did so.

My integrity as a private investigator and my ability to handle firearms had been questioned and debated in print, on television, and online all week. That wasn't what propelled me toward a career change. The chief had given a terse but kind sound bite about my help in cracking the case against Stern. The press had figured out Ric and I were living together, and they made a huge deal out of that. They'd somehow filmed us going up to the Palmer Park house for Sunday dinner, and even though you couldn't see our faces, the press always held a tight shot of our two hands, fingers entwined. Now the newscaster was saying something about Tupac Shakur.

"What?" I said aloud, sitting up. Photos of Madonna, who had grown up in the Detroit area, and Shakur, who had not, flashed on the screen. An apology letter Shakur had written to Madonna admitting he was breaking up with her because she was white was up for auction. In the letter, Shakur said he'd never meant to hurt her.

"I didn't even know they dated," I commented to Ric just as the reporter came back on camera, clearly trying to shoehorn my relationship with Ric into a similar pattern, saying, "We can exclusively report that Lily White has bought a combined residential and commercial property here in the city. Looks like this is the end of the romance between the police detective and the PI."

We both laughed. It was true, in a few days I'd be moving into a home of my own. But it was also true that this romance was just getting started, not ending.

Ric turned a little more toward me, took both my

hands in his. "I love you, and I'm not letting you go," he said. Then he kissed me in a way that could slay dragons. Well, it slayed me, anyway.

A word about the author…

Before retiring to write full time, I had a twenty-year career as an English teacher. I have been a staff reviewer for *Romantic Times* and *Publishers Weekly* and written features for popular magazines. I live in metro Detroit and St. Petersburg, Florida. *Lily White in Detroit* is my sixth novel with The Wild Rose Press.

Learn more on my website at
https://cynthiaharrison.com/

Thank you for purchasing
this publication of The Wild Rose Press, Inc.
For other wonderful stories,
please visit our on-line bookstore at
www.thewildrosepress.com.

For questions or more information
contact us at
info@thewildrosepress.com.

The Wild Rose Press, Inc.
www.thewildrosepress.com

To visit with authors of
The Wild Rose Press, Inc.
join our yahoo loop at
http://groups.yahoo.com/group/thewildrosepress/